Fallen Star

Also by Joan O'Neill

Daisy Chain War
Bread and Sugar
Daisy Chain Dream
Daisy Chain Days

Joan O'Neill

Fallen Star

Hodder
Children's
Books

a division of Hodder Headline Limited

Text copyright © 2005 Joan O'Neill

Published in Great Britain in 2005
by Hodder Children's Books

A Catalogue record for this book is available from
the British Library

ISBN 0 340 88179 8

Typeset in Bembo by Avon DataSet Ltd,
Bidford-on-Avon, Warwickshire

Printed and bound in Great Britain by
Clays Ltd, St Ives plc

The paper and board used in this paperback by Hodder Children's
Books are natural recyclable products made from wood grown in
sustainable forests. The manufacturing processes conform to the
environmental regulations of the country of origin.

Hodder Children's Books
A Division of Hodder Headline Limited
338 Euston Road
London NW1 3BH

For my sister, Marianne Gallagher,
who introduced me to the art of reading,
and my friend, Angela Farrell, who
urged me to write down my stories.

Prologue

1960

Leaving Knocknacree was the worst thing that I ever had to do. Though I was somewhere else, I never really left home. In my heart I was at the beach where the sky was always blue and the sun always shone, or I was chasing through the woods with Ciaran. Or sitting by the fireside with Mam, helping her with her sewing.

My name is Stella Wood and this is my story. I am sixteen years old and I had never been outside of Ireland, until recently. I grew up here, in Knocknacree, a small town in county Wicklow, with my father and my mother and my ten-year-old brother, Ciaran. Up until last year my life was uneventful, just a dreary round of school and home, then homework.

After Dad's job finished two years ago he went to work in England. We were all very sad when he left, but life went on as usual, until last spring when I met Charles Thornton. That's when everything changed.

It is hard to believe now that meeting Charles could

have led to such unforeseen events, and that an act that we were responsible for could cause such uproar and catastrophe. It is also hard to believe that I have come through it at all.

I remember the day Charles left the town. I clearly recall the spot where we stood whispering our goodbyes – the last lonely kiss, the last look over his shoulder. And I'll never forget the day that I left home: Father Cooney piling me into his little car and driving off, his jaws clenched. And the awful journey to Dublin to the Convent of the Blessed Wounds. I have only to close my eyes and I see that place rising up before me against a dark sky, and then I recall the terrible, long days and nights that followed.

One

April 1959

It was a Saturday afternoon and half an hour to closing time at the Coffee Pot, where I worked with my cousin Irene, the boss. A seafront café, it was one of the first to adopt the new coffee-making machines, and since it had opened in March it was already popular with the locals. Saturday was the busiest day and today was no exception. Irene was all hot and bothered, complaining that her feet were killing her. I'd been rushing around all day too, and I was tired, but I couldn't say that to her. She likes to throw her weight around. But behind her strict posture she's kind-hearted and well-meaning.

I took a swing of lemonade and went out front to clear up, leaving her in the Kitchen to cool down. That's when Charles Thornton and two other boys walked into the café and changed my life for ever.

With his dark good looks, Charles stood head and shoulders above his friends. As I served their table I glanced at him, wondering who he was. He looked familiar, but I couldn't place him. When he was leaving he tapped my arm. 'I'm Charles Thornton, I live at White House on Clover Hill. I'm having a party on Saturday night. Would you like to come? You can bring a friend if you like . . .'

I could barely meet the challenging look in his eager blue eyes, but a surge of excitement went through me. I had heard of the Thorntons, of course, everybody knew of them. They were one of the wealthiest families in Knocknacree – though it was the first time I found out where they lived. I struck what I hoped looked like a casual pose. 'Thanks,' I said casually. 'Maybe I will.' My heart was thudding.

He grinned triumphantly. 'That's great, see you about eight o'clock then.' He strode out with his pals, leaving me gazing after him.

Irene locked the door after the last customer and then turned and gave me a look.

'He's invited me to his party,' I told her.

Irene started cashing up. Her expression was tight-lipped. 'You shouldn't have encouraged him,' she said.

'I didn't.'

'I saw you giving him the glad eye. He's out of your league.'

'Just because he lives in that big house on the hill?' I laughed.

'According to Miss Kelly, Father Cooney's housekeeper, the Thorntons are Protestants. That makes them different to most of the folks around here,' she said, her eyes drilling into me. Her backcombed head bobbing, she continued: 'His father's a top-notch solicitor, his mother's one of the Savage Sweets people — they've got that big factory in Waterford. She's a bit of a snob with her posh accent, you'd swear she swallowed a dictionary.' Irene's tongue clicked disapprovingly.

'So what? It's only a party,' I said, far too happy to take any notice of her. It didn't matter to me who Charles Thornton's family was. If anything it made him all the more interesting.

After work I cycled to Maeve's house, my head spinning with excitement. Maeve lived next door to me in our narrow street of huddled-together cottages, called Station Row. We'd grown up together, had played with our dolls and prams in each other's houses. We'd learned to skip at the same time, had played hopscotch and marbles on the street. We still did our homework together sometimes; dressed up in each other's clothes, and experimented with our mothers' lipstick and powder. Maeve was like a sister to me. She still is.

I threw my bike against her hedge and raced round to her open back door. Mrs Ruane was getting the tea in the kitchen. 'Hello, Stella,' she said with a big smile. 'Were you busy today?' she asked.

'Busiest so far,' I said. 'Where's Maeve?'

'She's down the back, collecting the eggs. Want a cup of tea? I was just about to make a pot.'

'No thanks, Mrs Ruane.'

I ran down the garden path calling, 'Maeve?'

She stuck her head out of the hen house door. 'Stella? What's up?'

'Guess what? This good-looking fella came into the café today and invited me to his birthday party, and he said to bring a friend. His name is Charles Thornton,' I gabbled, my voice high with excitement. 'He lives in that beautiful big house on Clover Hill, the one that we're always admiring.'

Maeve gulped. The hens squawked. 'So *he* lives there does he? Wonder what it's like inside?' She was more curious about the house than she was about the party.

'Well. we'll find out on Saturday – not that I care about the house, I'm only interested in Charles.'

'Isn't he the one Mary Brown likes?' Maeve smiled mischievously.

'I couldn't care less about Mary Brown,' I said nonchalantly.

Maeve guffawed. 'Not half.'

'All the same we'd better keep this to ourselves; if she finds out she'll try and muscle in, you'll see.'

We burst out laughing.

The truth was I was a bit scared of Mary Brown, as were most of the other girls in my class. She was our class prefect, a big bossy-boots, full of her own importance. She prowled around our school like a leopard on a leash, her boot-button eyes missing nothing, her mean mouth yapping out orders, her arms drilling into us if she caught us out of line. She liked nothing better than to catch us smoking a woodbine behind the bicycle shed, or having a sneaky read of the *True Romance* magazines Kathleen Long brought in. Mary's parents were the big drapers in the town and she thought she owned the place. Because Mam worked for the Browns, Mary lorded it over me the most. She was my sworn enemy.

When Maeve's tea was ready, I went home next door and found Mam at the stove, frying rashers and sausages.

'How did you get on today?' she asked, turning to give me a quick smile. When I told her about the party invitation she looked up in surprise. 'Socialising with the Thorntons no less!'

'Do you know them?'

'I've made a suit for Mrs Thornton. They're friends of the Browns, and very important people in the town.'

'I suppose stupid Mary will be invited to the party too,' I sighed.

Mam looked at me. 'I hope you'll conduct yourself properly, Stella?'

'You know I will, Mam.'

'Can I come with you?' Ciaran, my little brother, asked coming into the kitchen as soon as he heard the word 'party'.

'No, silly, you're too young,' I laughed, tousling his hair.

'Does Charles know that we live on Station Row?' Mam asked.

'I don't think so. What difference does it make?'

'None I suppose.'

Our house is the end one and the prettiest. The front door and sash windows are painted green. Fine lace curtains veil the windows. In summer the path is bordered with flowers: geraniums, dog daisies, and clumps of forget-me-nots. The long back garden has a high wall, where Ciaran bounces his ball for hours at a time. I was proud of our street, and wished that Mam were too. But she aspired to better for our family.

Behind the houses is the disused railway station. Purple rhododendrons grow along the embankment; grass covers the rows of rusted sleepers. Leaning trees block the overgrown path to the platform. Stray willow branches reach down over the dilapidated ticket office, whose dirty windows peer up toward endless fields of hedgerows and trees that stretch to the hills.

The houses on Station Row originally belonged to Coras Lompar Eireann, the state bus and train service. They had employed Dad from the age of fourteen. He used to speak of the firm with reverence, as if it was a rich, distant uncle that he was in awe of, until he was made redundant. After that he didn't speak of it at all, even though CLE had let us buy our house cheaply from them and had given Dad enough money to do so in his redundancy package.

Turning back to Mam I said, 'I'd love something new to wear to the party.'

'I'll make you a frock, I've got some nice new material,' she said. 'Now tell Ciaran to come in for his tea, and to wash his hands.'

After tea she went to her big steamer trunk in the corner, where she kept her personal treasures, and raised the curved lid. She lifted out the top tray, with its wallpapered sections packed with precious tissue-wrapped trinkets, and placed it on the floor; then she reached in and brought out her stock of remnants. Throwing out the lengths of colourful material she said, 'Which one would you like?'

I picked out the latest 'Gigi' print in tangerine glazed cotton.

Mam draped the lovely material over the open trunk, pinched it in at the sides. 'Good choice. Now I wonder what style would suit you best? You're getting so tall,' she said, looking at me proudly. She took out her pattern books. There was nothing that I liked among them, so on the back page of my copybook I made a quick sketch of a frock I'd seen in a magazine. It had a billowy skirt with a streamer bow at the back, and a deep, stiffened belt trimmed the waist.

Thoughtful, she studied it. 'Yes, I see. You'll look beautiful in that, Stella.'

'Thanks Mam,' I said, giving her a quick hug.

Mam was a gifted seamstress. She had trained as a

dressmaker in Dublin city, where she grew up, and was now head seamstress for Browns. She made all our clothes. Often she sewed late into the night. I loved to sit and watch her expert fingers guiding the material down the neat line of stitching, as the shuttle raced back and forth. She would stop only to change the dial of her radio that kept her company.

Mam had made covers for our armchairs and sofa from the plush red material Auntie Nora, her sister, had given her. She even made a lampshade for our standard lamp and trimmed it with gold tassels.

Brown's is the biggest and smartest shop in town with its fashionable, double-fronted window display. In her spare time, not that she had much of it, Mam made clothes for a few private clients: well-heeled ladies who occasionally came to our house for fittings. Tonight was my turn.

Mam had me standing for hours while she pinned material around me for a pattern. Finally, she declared she had the perfect fit and got to work just as I was going to bed. Later that night I lay in bed listening to the whirr-whirr of her sewing machine, and the thump of the treadle as her feet powered it in a fearful frenzy, too excited to sleep. Exhaustion finally took me over.

The sun shining through the window roused me. I crept into the kitchen. Sunlight glowed from the sides of the kitchen curtains – just enough light to see the lovely dress Mam had made.

Mam came into the kitchen. 'Try it on,' she said.

It fitted like a glove. I ran my fingers down the smooth folds that flowed from the waistline, too choked up to talk.

'Do you like it?' she asked.

'It's beautiful, Mam, thank you,' I said, giving her a hug.

'I'll bring home netting this evening, to stiffen the skirt. It'll be real fancy when it's finished.' Pleased with her night's work she pushed back a few strands of hair from my forehead. 'You'll be the belle of the ball,' she said, before turning to the stove to cook the porridge.

'Why can't I go to the party too?' Ciaran groaned.

'Oh, don't start that again.' Mam placed a bowl of porridge on the table in front of him. Although he was nine years old Ciaran was small for his age, and Mam, worried about his slow growth, tried to feed him up.

'It's not fair,' he went on.

Placing her hands gently on his cheeks she said, 'Stop moithering, I'll take you to the pictures if you eat your breakfast. A treat.' Mam fussed much more over Ciaran now that Dad wasn't there to take him places. Ciaran missed him terribly. We all did.

Dad is a tall, quiet, good-humoured man who was always joking and teasing us, the opposite of serious Mam with her mood swings. Her quick hugs followed by sudden bursts of anger often left us feeling confused. It was Dad who'd decided that my name should be Estelle. He called me his 'Little Star'. Sometimes he called me his 'Rising Star'. He knew the names of all the stars in the galaxy, and he would tell us them. He would draw for us too, sometimes: birds of all varieties, and puppies and kittens with long tails, his pencil flying across the page. At night, when we were tucked up in bed, he would tell us stories about his childhood on his family's farm in County Wexford. He knew all about flowers and crops. He knew which mushrooms you could eat and which were poisonous.

Dad had worked on the railways all of his life, starting out as a railway tracker when he was just a boy, rising to the position of stationmaster. He loved the railway and he believed in it passionately. That's why he was so upset when the government closed down our station. He hated the system that he said had cut off our town from the rest of the county because, according to them, it was uneconomical to keep it going.

I'd loved the railway when I was younger. On sunny afternoons Maeve and I would sit on our back wall, overlooking the railway station, and wait for the arrival of each train. There were two trains on weekdays, one in the morning and one in the evening. It was mostly workers in the town who came by the early train, except in summer when swarms of day-trippers would arrive. I loved the slow grinding sound as the train drew into the station, and the shrill blow of Dad's whistle, then his voice, clear and friendly in the morning air. Mothers laden down with picnic baskets, kettles tied to them, and children with buckets and spades would stream out on to the platform, eager to get to the beach for the best of the sunshine.

The evening train was full of local people, their familiar faces gaunt and tired from a day's work in Wicklow town. Dad would always take a minute or two to talk to them. He would crack jokes with them; other times he would listen, tenderness in the nod of his head as they poured out their hearts to him. If a regular passenger were in trouble he would listen to their anguished voices, his face full of sympathy, and speak to them in his soft murmur that I always connected to the station. He understood them and cared about them. I used to wonder why he often found it difficult to be patient with Mam when he was so patient with strangers. She used to say that he knew his customers too well, and she often criticised him for being too familiar with them.

Often, we would wait in the ticket office for the Wexford-bound train and watch travellers drop pennies, sixpenny pieces, and shillings into the hole through the half-closed window. As soon as the train had left the station we would dash out to search for a big, brown penny or a thrupenny bit that may have slipped through frail fingers.

Sometimes Dad would have a treat for us in the evenings when he came home. It might be a bar of chocolate, or a box of colouring pencils, or drawing paper. Once he gave me a doll wrapped in a brown-paper parcel that had been left for ages in Lost Property. I was thrilled, but I often wondered whom she'd really been meant for when I played with her.

After the station shut, it seemed as if the rest of the town followed in sympathy. The only hotel closed down and the owner fled to America. Small businesses closed their books. There were no jobs. Dad tried his best to find another position somewhere, but he wasn't trained for anything else but the railway. He helped his brother – Irene's dad, Uncle Tom – out on the farm, and did odd jobs here and there, but not enough money was coming in. Dad lost hope of ever getting anything permanent in Knocknacree and eventually he went to England to work for a building firm. Though the separation from him was very difficult, Mam being a good Catholic accepted that it was the will of God.

The day he left, Dad carried Ciaran up on his shoulders to the bus stop, and promised him that if he didn't cry he would send him a cowboy outfit in the post. Then he kissed me on the cheek and told me to take care of Mam. He kept his arm around Mam for ages as he said goodbye to her. Before he boarded the bus he glanced quickly back, his eyes taking us in, then he got on. We waved and kept waving until the bus was out of sight. We knew we wouldn't be seeing him for a long time to come.

When Dad went, his magic went with him. He wrote

to us regularly at first. Mick, the postman, brought a letter in a brown envelope every single Monday morning, with a five-pound note enclosed between the folds of thin notepaper full of neat handwriting. As time went on he wrote less and less news. Mam said that it almost seemed as if he was forgetting us. I knew he wasn't because the money arrived every single week without fail, 'with love and kisses' scrawled across the page it was wrapped in.

During the following week I made myself too busy to have much time to think about Charles and the party. I took Ciaran to school each morning, then crossed the road to the secondary school.

The Sisters of Mercy nuns ran the National primary and secondary schools, beyond the town. The nuns were strict, but I liked school. I liked Sister Gabriel, the headmistress and our English teacher. She always encouraged me to study hard, with the promise of a bright future if I did so. My secret ambition was to become a famous film star, like Leslie Caron in the film *Lili*. I didn't tell anyone, not even Maeve, for fear she would laugh at me.

In the evenings I did my homework, and minded Ciaran until Mam got home from work. I even helped Mam sew buttons on a cashmere coat she had made for Mrs Brown. I liked sewing. I was good at it. But as the week drew to a close I found myself counting the hours until Saturday.

Two

On Saturday morning I woke up early, with a feeling of nervous excitement in the pit of my stomach. The feeling stayed with me all through a busy day at the café and didn't get any better with Irene's teasing. I finally escaped at five o'clock and raced home quickly to get ready. After a long bath, I put on my frock, smoothing the material over the netting, liking how it rustled when it moved and seemed to promise me happiness for ever. I wore the high heels my Auntie Nora had sent me for Christmas. Slowly, I put on eye-shadow and lipstick and a little of Mam's cream puff powder, then I went into her bedroom to look in her long mirror. I was surprised at how good I looked. I felt really glamorous, almost beautiful. This feeling lasted all the way to the party.

Maeve loved my new frock. 'You're a bit of a daredevil,' she said, when she saw the scooped neckline.

'It's the latest fashion,' I said, doing a pirouette outside Mrs Cribbins' house. Maeve's next-door neighbour peered out from behind her twitching curtains, her scandalised eyebrows raised.

The Thorntons' house was at the end of a long drive, with wide lawns on either side, the surrounding trees strung with fairy lights. Light streamed from the windows. The front door was open and music floated out. Coming up the drive we could hear Elvis Presley begging us not to step on his blue suede shoes.

'It's very grand,' Maeve said under her breath as I rang the doorbell.

Charles came into the hall. 'Hello,' he said with a smile, ushering us inside, his voice drowning in the noise. In a black suit, white shirt and thin black tie, his hair slicked, he looked even more handsome; like a man, and not the carefree boy of the previous week.

In the sitting room the carpet was rolled back, the furniture pushed against the wall. Boys stood around talking; some of them we knew by sight, and some of them were strangers. At the opposite end of the room strange girls stood in a group, chatting to one another, making a point of ignoring the boys.

While Charles went to get our drinks, Maeve and I skirted around pretending that we couldn't care less about the boys. Mary Brown appeared in a hideous, tight green dress that made her look as big as a heifer. Her exaggerated pencilled-in eyebrows rose even higher when she saw us.

'What are you doing here?' she asked rudely.

'Charles invited us,' Maeve said haughtily.

Mary stormed off, her noise out of joint. It was obvious

16

that she was only there because of her parents' standing in the town.

Charles was in the corner sorting through a stack of records, scrutinising the labels. The Crickets burst out with 'That'll Be The Day', one of my favourite tunes. Some of the boys and girls started to move about to the music. Charles came over to me and asked me to dance. I was glad the lights were turned low so that he couldn't see me blush as I took his outstretched hand and went into the centre of the floor.

'Let yourself go,' he said, jiving to the beat. We bobbed and swayed; he swung me round. Laughing at his antics, I did all the moves that Maeve and I'd been practising.

'Hey, you're good at this,' he said, ducking me under his arm.

'Buddy Holly's my idol,' I told him.

'He's one of my favourites too,' he said.

'Every Day' came next. Charles sang along, blending his voice with Buddy's special mixture of confidence, uncertainty, and hope. *'Ev'ry day . . . it's-a-gettin' closer . . . goin' faster than a rollercoaster . . . love like yours will surely come my way . . .'* As Buddy's guitar broke into a crescendo at the end of the song, Charles looked down at me with a brilliant, careless smile, his mood matching the mood of the song. We stayed close together, not looking at one another.

Someone put on 'Peggy Sue' and Mary Brown came stalking towards us. 'Would you like to dance, Charles?'

she asked boldly, giving him a flirtatious look and me a filthy one.

I just smiled, hiding my annoyance, while Charles had impeccable manners. 'Of course,' he smiled, and with a polite, 'Excuse me,' he was gone.

I sought out Maeve.

'He likes you, I can tell,' she said.

'I hope so,' I said, my eyes on stupid Mary Brown lumbering round the floor.

A boy then asked Maeve to dance and, feeling conspicuous, I made my way to the bathroom. When I got back the floor was packed, everyone dancing like mad. I couldn't see Charles anywhere.

When Leo, a neighbour of mine, asked me to dance, I practically fell into his arms with gratitude.

'Good party,' he said, looking out to the hall, where the dancing had extended.

'Terrific. How come you know Charles?'

'We're on the same rugby team,' he said.

The Platters sang 'Smoke Gets In Your Eyes', and Charles returned to claim me. Drawing me to him, his arm tight around me, his cheek against mine, we danced slowly. I forgot about everything. It was just Charles and I.

As soon as the song ended a tall, pretty woman I took to be Mrs Thornton announced that supper was served in the dining room.

Here, there was a long sideboard full of dainty assorted

sandwiches, sausage rolls, and crackers with a dab of anchovy and salmon on each one. There was trifle in an enormous bowl, topped with hundreds and thousands, iced cakes in paper cases, pink wafer biscuits, afternoon-tea biscuits, and a huge iced cake in the middle of it all, with seventeen candles on it waiting to be lit.

We all lined up with our plates. Mrs Thornton told us to help ourselves. I took a sandwich and a sausage roll. As I passed by Mrs Thornton she leaned towards me and said in a lovely voice, 'Have some more, that's hardly enough.' The scent of her perfume mingled with the smell of the delicious food she put on my plate.

I tried to think of something sophisticated to say to impress her but all that came out was, 'That's plenty thank you.'

I followed Maeve to the end of the room, where we found chairs to sit on. Out of the corner of my eye I noticed Mary Brown watching me. With a mocking expression she said, 'You'll get fat if you eat all that.' I was about to react when I remembered Mam's advice to act like a lady at all times, so I stuck my head in the air and pretended not to hear her. I was having far too good a time to bother about what she said.

There was loud cheering when Charles blew out his candles all in one go, and everyone sang 'Happy Birthday'.

Soon the dancing began again with 'Rock Around The Clock'. We were all up on the floor, rocking and jiving. When the lullaby voice of Pat Boone began 'I'll Remember Tonight,' Charles danced with me again. I could feel his breath on my face as he moved closer. Pressing me to him he said, 'I'll remember tonight always.' Our eyes locked. I was about to say that I would too, when he put his finger to my lips and, wrapping his arms around me, he pulled me even closer. Resting my head on his shoulder I wished I could stay like that for ever, but I knew that soon this magical night would have to end.

Next, Elvis sang 'Love Me Tender'. We clung together, barely moving. When the music stopped I broke away from him reluctantly. 'I have to go, I'll be killed if I'm home late,' I said.

'I'll give you a lift on my new motorbike,' he said, kissing the side of my mouth and making my heart leap. I began to protest that I couldn't leave Maeve to get home by herself, but she appeared with a couple of school friends she'd spotted and assured me that she would get a lift with them.

'So. No excuses, Stella.' Charles smiled and took my hand. He led me out into the dark, cool air and the front of the house, where his shiny motorbike, a birthday present from his parents, was parked. Handing me a spare helmet, he put on his, then proudly threw one leg astride the seat, and kick-started the engine. Flexing his wrists, he pushed off with one foot. Gripping the handlebars, he indicated to me to jump on. Soon we were out on the road roaring along, me clinging to him tightly, terrified as the cold air rushed through my lungs.

'Relax,' he called over his shoulder.

I loosened my grip, but kept my thighs pressed against him as the wheels beneath us bounced along the rutted road. By the time we reached my street I was wishing the journey could have lasted longer.

I scrambled off, my legs aching, while he parked at the corner so as not to wake up the neighbours. Silently, he walked me to my house. At the gate I thanked him for the party.

'I'm so glad you enjoyed it,' he smiled as we stood close.

'I'd better go in,' I said, suddenly awkward. 'Goodnight.'

'Goodnight,' he said. In that split second my whole body tingled, longing for his touch once more. But instead he took a step backwards, saying, 'I'll see you.'

'See you.' I watched him walk away. I wanted to call out to him, run after him, but I knew better.

As I reached into the letterbox for the string with the door key on it, I heard a soft, 'Stella?'

I turned. He'd doubled back, and was walking towards me.

I went to him. Shyly, he said, in a low voice, 'Would you like to go to the cinema next Saturday night?'

'I'd love to,' I said, unable to hide my delight.

'I'll see you in the café, Saturday after work then?'

'Great.'

He walked quickly away. I watched his dark solid shape move in the black night, heard the sound of his motorbike revving up and taking off, then I let myself in and crept into bed. For a long time I lay staring into the darkness, my head spinning as I thought of the night and all the songs we'd danced to. Shivers ran down my spine and into my toes as I remembered the feel of Charles's fingertip on my cheek and the touch of his lips against the side of my mouth, like the caress of a butterfly. My heart swelled up inside me at the prospect of our date. Finally I fell asleep.

When I woke up the next morning the house was quiet. I got up, dressed quickly in my Sunday frock, ate my breakfast, and went to call Maeve for mass to avoid Mam's questioning eyes.

'So, tell me . . .' Maeve said, her eyes like bullets of curiosity as she riddled me with questions. She was bursting to know everything. I described Charles's motorbike, his helmet, and the journey home.

'But did he kiss you?' she asked, her voice blunt with impatience.

'No, not properly,' I said, trying not to sound disappointed.

She looked surprised. 'Why not?'

'I don't know,' I said, embarrassed.

After mass Mary Brown spied us and rushed over. 'So, you cadged a lift off Charles Thornton last night,' she said to me, unable to keep the resentment out of her voice.

22

'What's it to you?' I snapped at her.

Maeve shot me a look. I could tell she was wondering where I'd got the courage to speak to Mary like that.

'Nothing, only you'd want to watch yourself with him. He doesn't care about anyone but himself.'

'And how would you know?' I retorted hotly.

'Never you mind. Don't say I didn't warn you,' Mary said, wagging her finger at me as if I was a child before she sauntered off.

'Why did she say that?' I asked Maeve on the way home. 'Do you think she knows something about him that we don't?'

' 'Course not. She's just being her nasty self. Take no notice of her, she's jealous,' Maeve assured me.

The following Saturday the café was already packed when I got there. Irene was juggling a million tasks at once. 'I don't know what would have happened if you hadn't come this minute,' she said. 'Mrs Tighe wants a boiled egg and toast, and they want coffee over there.'

I rushed around, too busy to think of anything except serving the customers, until the evening, when two of Charles's friends came in and sat huddled into a corner table, heads close as they argued the toss over the outcome of the rugby match they'd just played. There was no sign of Charles. When Leo came in I asked him if he'd seen him.

'Stella, can't you see that we're mad busy? Ed Brown,

by the door there, wants coffee,' Irene called out above the high voices of the customers and the hiss of the coffee machine. I rushed away to serve Ed, Mary's brother, without getting my answer. I kept moving, clearing tables until the last customer left, and then I was instructed to wash the floor.

Finally I raced home on my bike to get ready for my date, and hurried to the cinema. Outside, I waited for what seemed like hours, but was only minutes, terrified that Charles wouldn't turn up. Then I heard the roar of a motorbike and turned to see him flying down the hill towards me, his motorbike glittering in the evening sunlight. My heart leaped with delight.

'Sorry I'm late,' he said, when he'd parked. 'My mother isn't well, I had to get the doctor for her.'

'Oh dear. Is she very sick?' I asked, concerned.

He shook his head. 'She's got some kind of flu bug, but she'll be all right. Dad's home now so he'll look after her. Was the café busy?' he asked.

'It was bedlam. I thought I'd never get away.'

Charles pretended not to see his friends winking at one another as we joined the queue to see Marilyn Monroe in *Some like It Hot*. In the cinema he took my hand and held it tight as Marilyn sang and pranced around in a tight-fitting dress. Her fantastic figure made me think of my own meagre chest and thin lips, and wonder what Charles could possibly see in me.

When it was over we trailed out into the warm

evening, full of happy chatter about the film. Charles bought fish and chips, which we ate dawdling down to the beach. It was quiet there; the only noise was the swish of the waves against the rocks as the tide heaved in. We crunched along the pebbly sand, licked the vinegar from our fingers, and burst our paper bags with loud bangs that set sleeping seagulls squawking in protest. We skimmed stones, watched them ricochet off the water; then, taking off his jacket, Charles spread it out in a sheltered spot, under a boulder. I felt the wind in my hair as I sat down beside him. We huddled close together and talked. Charles told me that he missed Galway city, where he'd grown up. He said that he hated being an only child; that apart from being lonely, it made him the centre of his parents' attention, which was not a good thing according to him, because they expected too much from him. I looked at him, taken aback. I hadn't imagined that someone like Charles Thornton could feel lonely.

'What will you do when the leaving certificate is over?' I asked him.

'I'd like to take a year out to travel, see the world, and enjoy myself before I decide.'

'Oh! That would be fun,' I said, my heart sinking.

'Dad's not keen on the idea. He wants me to study architecture and build big modern offices in the city, make loads of money.'

'Wouldn't you like that?'

'Maybe, but not yet. I don't want to be tied down.' And behind his smile and kind eyes I detected a wild streak. 'How about you? What do you want to do with your life?' he asked.

'Promise you won't laugh if I tell you,' I said, suddenly shy.

'Cross my heart and hope to die,' he said solemnly.

I told him about my dream of becoming a film star. He listened in rapt attention, his arm around me. 'You've certainly got the looks,' he said, moving closer. Then, turning, he kissed me. His warm lips sent shivers down my spine. Trembling, my heart racing, I confided in him that I'd never been kissed before. He laughed, curled into me and kissed me again, pressing his strong body against mine. I lay back and gazed up at the sky, and the squalling seagulls, feeling a rush of joy as he kissed me again. Wrapped up in his arms I felt completely happy until I suddenly remembered the time, and that I'd promised Mam I wouldn't be too late home.

'I've got to go,' I said. 'Mam'll be wondering where I am.'

'Already? It's only half past nine.'

'I have to be in by ten or I'll be in trouble.'

Hand in hand we crunched across the stones and, passing a poster advertising the forthcoming circus on a lamppost, the pictures illustrating the face of a laughing clown, Charles asked if I'd like to go to the circus the following week.

'I'd love it, but Ciaran will be disappointed if I don't go with him.'

'Bring him along too.'

'Could I?'

'Of course. It'll be fun.'

'That'd be great, he'd love it.'

'I'll call for you both at two o'clock,' he said, and with a quick peck on the cheek he was gone.

Three

On Monday morning, on the way to school, I tried telling Maeve all about the film we'd seen but she only wanted to know about Charles. 'He must have kissed you by now,' she said, looking at me quizzically.

'What do you think?' I laughed.

'What was it like? I'm dying to know.' Her eager eyes swept my face.

Giggling, I told her that it was the most amazing thing that had ever happened to me. 'And guess what? He's taking Ciaran and me to the circus.'

'You lucky thing,' she said, enviously.

In school Mary was waiting for me, a spiteful smile on her face. 'Saw you and Charles Thornton down on the beach,' she taunted me. 'Quite the lovebirds, aren't you.'

I felt my cheeks redden.

'He's trouble, you know that, don't you.' she said smugly.

'Why were you spying on me?' I said, my rising temper giving me a false sense of courage.

'I wasn't spying. I just happened to be walking by.'

I swung round. 'You're just jealous,' I said and walked off.

She came after me. 'I'll have to report you to Sister Gabriel for cheek and insubordination if you keep this up,' she said threateningly.

I shook my head, rolling my eyes to heaven. Though I feared Sister Gabriel's wrath, as did all the girls at school, Mary wouldn't have the nerve to report me to her. I was sure of it. But still, I decided to avoid the spiteful girl as much as possible from now on.

The following Sunday afternoon, Charles collected us in his father's car and drove us to the circus at the outskirts of the town. Ciaran couldn't contain his excitement, leaping around in the back seat and plaguing Charles with questions about the car.

The big tent was erected in a sheltered corner of Noonan's field. People who had come from towns and villages queued up patiently. There were jugglers and a fire-eater who would have set himself aflame if it hadn't been for the clown who strutted forth and squirted him with water from his bagpipes. From our seats in the front row we had the best view of acrobats performing amazing feats on tightropes, dancing ponies galloping round the ring – sequinned dancers tumbling through golden hoops on their backs. The last pony refused to perform. The ringmaster, in a red coat and top hat, cracked his whip but it was no use. Jeering broke out as the pony walked to Ciaran and nudged his lollipop out of his hand. Ciaran squealed as the crowd shrieked with laughter.

On the way out a Spanish fortune teller with a black mantilla draped over her face stopped us by her tent. 'Cross my palm with silver, and I'll tell you your future,' she said in a heavily accented voice.

Charles tossed her a shilling.

Inside her candlelit cavern she took my right hand and gazed at it. 'You will walk down zee wrong path and you will pay zee price.' I laughed at her, but she gripped my hand tighter, and looking into my eyes said, 'Your life will come good. You will get your wish. One day you will shine like a star.'

I couldn't believe what I was hearing. I was going to be a film star, living in Hollywood perhaps. Overjoyed, I decided to keep this prediction to myself because nobody would believe it.

Charles sent Ciaran to buy three ice cream cones while we browsed at a stall full of useless china ornaments. At another stall there was a display of colourful jewellery and trinkets. We stopped to have a look.

'Would you like that?' Charles said, pointing to a beautiful silver charm bracelet.

'It's lovely, but it's not my birthday or anything,' I said.

Smiling, he bought the bracelet. 'Call it a keepsake,' he said, putting it round my wrist and clasping it shut.

'Thank you,' I said, touching the tiny St. Christopher charm, then the starfish and the cross linked to the chain, hardly believing my good fortune.

Ciaran returned with the ice cream cones and the change. He ate his running on ahead, in his excitement to get to the car first.

Outside the house, Ciaran thanked him and ran in to tell Mam all about his day out. Charles refused to come in and meet Mam, saying that he had to go home to study.

'Thanks Charles. We had a great time,' I said.

'So did I.' Just as I was getting out of the car he said, 'Listen, why don't you come to my house for tea, next Saturday after work. The folks will be away.'

'Oh, I don't think . . .'

'Bridie, the housekeeper, will be there — if that's what you're worried about.'

'OK, then.' I got out of the car.

'Great.' Then with a wave he was gone, leaving me no time to change my mind.

Charles answered the door as soon as I knocked on it. I could hardly breathe with excitement as he brought me into the kitchen, where Bridie was preparing tea. 'Nice to see you,' she said, putting two plates of ham salad on a silver tray.

Charles took me into the sitting room.

'This is a lovely room,' I said, admiring the deep cream

upholstery on the sofas and chairs, and the pale yellow curtains that looked so different in the daylight. 'You're spoilt living in a house like this, with a housekeeper to see to your every need,' I teased him.

'Yes, I'm lucky, I suppose,' he said, though his expression was sad.

We ate our meal sitting by the fire, listening to Buddy and the Crickets singing 'Maybe Baby'. Bridie brought in a pot of tea, and said that she was off to the Novena and then to her sister's. I would be alone with Charles.

We talked about music – about Buddy Holly, who had died earlier in the year. About how shocking it was for his fans worldwide, and about the useless waste of such a wonderful, talented young life.

' "All My Love" is my favourite song,' I told Charles, who played it, and we sang along giggling at the same time.

At half past nine I told Charles that I'd better be going. 'Just ten minutes longer . . .'

I finally made a move towards the door at ten o'clock, reluctant to tear myself away from him, hating to spoil the feeling of closeness we were sharing.

Charles pulled the curtains with a swish, turned on the lamps, then stepped towards me. His eyes glowed in the light as he took me in his arms and kissed me. My knees swayed, the blood rushed to my head as we sank into the sofa, our bodies pressed together. While Buddy sang 'Peggy Sue' we kissed over and over again.

'Charles! We shouldn't be doing this,' I said breathlessly, pushing him away.

'Why?'

'Anyone could walk in.'

He smiled. 'Bridie won't be back for hours, but we can go upstairs if you'd feel more comfortable.'

Taking me by the hand he led me up to his bedroom. Both excited and frightened by his spontaneity and daring, and overwhelmed by the powerful feelings I had for him, I felt out of control, unable to stop myself, and I let him make love to me. I knew it was wrong, but afterwards, Charles took me in his arms. 'You OK?' he asked, pulling me closer to him.

'Yes,' I said, for a while content in his tender embrace. We both lay in silence for a while. Eventually I said, 'It's late.'

Charles gave a heartfelt sigh. 'I wish you could stay the night.'

'I wish I could too, but I'd better go before Mam has the cops out searching for me.' We looked at each other and smiled. Reluctantly Charles got to his feet, straightened his shirt, and combed his hair while I dressed and put on my shoes.

Charles dropped me off at the corner of our street. He gave me a hug, squeezing me tightly. Just as we pulled apart he said, 'See you soon.'

Mam was sitting in her chair listening to the radio. The sight of her broad shoulders in her floral dress, her solid back, and the bow of her apron tied round her waist sent such a longing for comfort in me that I wanted to run to her, lay my head on her shoulder and say, 'Hold me, Mam, never let me go.' But the face she turned to me was frosty.

'You're late again, what kept you?' she asked crossly.

'I forgot the time. We were all down on the beach and . . .'

Her eyes cut through me. 'You and who else?'

'Maeve, Leo and Charles and . . .'

Her face tightened. 'That's a lie. Maeve was out in her back garden not an hour ago.' Mam's lips pursed in anger. 'I don't know what's got into you lately, young lady, but this had better stop.' Her shoulders drooped suddenly. She looked defeated. 'You have your studies to think about, you know.'

'Sorry Mam.' I looked at her, not knowing what else to say.

'Don't let it happen again,' she said gruffly.

'I won't,' I promised her, and went to bed where I tossed and turned, sleepless, while Ciaran slept soundly next door. I'd always seen my bedroom as a comforting place, but suddenly it was dark and full of haunting guilt. Worse than the guilt was a deep sense of shame of what I'd done with Charles. I had committed a mortal sin, and I would have to confess it to a priest before the following Sunday because Mam would become suspicious if I weren't at the altar rails to receive Holy Communion as usual.

★ ★ ★

Next day, on our way into school, I told Maeve.

'You did IT!' she exclaimed in astonishment.

'Shh.'

She looked around, smiling. 'There's nobody about.'

'What was it like?' she asked excitedly. 'Was it exactly like it is in the books, all romantic and wonderful?'

'No. It was . . .' I was about to say 'disappointing,' but I felt disloyal to Charles. I really wished I could have told her that it had been an amazing experience, but I couldn't lie to her. 'It wasn't what I expected,' I confided to her. 'It was over so quickly. And it's a sin, Maeve, a mortal one. How am I going to confess it?'

'Pleasure is always sinful, according to the nuns,' Maeve said flatly. 'But it's not the worst sin in the world, there are bigger ones.'

I knew she was trying to make me feel better but it didn't work.

Maeve peered at me. 'Did Charles make you do it?'

'Oh no, we got carried away, that's all,' I said, ashamed and bewildered by the whole experience.

'Doesn't sound anything like the passionate night in *Angelique and the Sultan*,' Maeve sighed.

'It wasn't.'

'We'll have to get a book on biology out of the library and read up on the subject,' she said cheerfully.

'Don't tell anyone. Mam would be scandalised if she ever found out.'

'I wouldn't dream of it,' Maeve said. 'Anyway, it's not that big a deal,' she added, knowing it was.

The following Saturday at five o'clock, Charles came into the café and greeted me as if nothing out of the ordinary had happened. When I'd finished for the day, we went for a walk along the deserted beach and found a place to sit, looking at the sea. Charles talked about his forthcoming exams. With a sigh he said, 'I'll have to study hard and pass my exams – then I'm going to get away from this place.' His eyes were staring ahead as if he was desperately searching for somewhere to go to.

'Where to?' I asked.

'I don't know, another country perhaps?' He said it as if it was a challenge to anyone who would try to stop him.

I looked up at him. His eyes were half closed and there were dark shadows beneath them. It seemed impossible to me that he could want to be anywhere but in Knocknacree at that moment. A cold breeze rose up. I pulled my cardigan across my chest and curled into him. He put his arm around me. There was stillness all around the desolate beach, as if Charles had already left. Reading my thoughts he said, 'There must be more to life than studying. I want to know what's going on in other places. There's a different world out there, Stella, one we know nothing about. I haven't made up my mind about where to go yet . . .'

There was a slight hesitation in his voice, as if he was wondering if he had said too much.

'Well, I won't stop you,' I said, turning my face away, keeping my eyes on the sky and the clouds that drifted past.

He yawned and stretched back.

'I've got to go home. I'll be in trouble if I'm late again,' I said, getting up.

This time Charles didn't protest. We went home along the path by the old railway tracks, Charles leading the way along the embankment. At the end of our road he lingered, reluctant to release me from his grasp.

'Would you like to go to the matinée tomorrow?' he asked.

'I have to mind Ciaran. Mam's going on a parish outing to Knock shrine,' I said, disappointed.

'He can come too – it'll be fun. Like the circus,' Charles said cheerfully.

On Sunday afternoon we held hands through the film, *Rio Bravo*, with John Wayne and Dean Martin, while the kids in the front rows made a racket – Ciaran the noisiest of all of them. Afterwards, the three of us walked through the new housing estate behind the station, Ciaran daring us to climb up the scaffolding with him. Charles hauled him back down, then saw us to the corner of our street. I invited him in for tea but he declined again, saying that he had to be home to study.

'I'll see you Saturday,' he promised, and gave me a quick kiss in the shelter of the doorway.

The following Saturday he came into the Coffee Pot with some of his friends. He looked drawn and anxious and the light had left his eyes. He talked about the forthcoming exams with dread, and told me he had to go home to study.

I didn't see much of him in the days and weeks after that, and I wondered what had gone wrong. I couldn't sleep, couldn't do my homework. I snapped at Ciaran. In school I got into an argument with Mary Brown when she said Charles had just used me and moved on to another girl.

'He's studying,' I said defensively, inwardly panicking that she was right.

'Charles Thornton, studying? That'll be the day,' she scoffed.

Maeve said to her, 'And how come you know so much about him, Mary?'

'Wouldn't you like to know,' she said, pointing to her nose.

Four

One morning I woke up feeling sick and dizzy. In the kitchen Mam peered at me, 'You're as white as a ghost.' With a worried frown she examined my tongue and gently pulled down the skin under my eye to expose the red flesh under the rim. 'You're run-down,' she declared. 'You're not getting enough sleep.'

I straightened up, the dizziness passed. 'I'm all right now.'

She went into the pantry to get milk to put in bottles for our lunch, saying, 'It's all that work at the café.'

'I only work on Saturdays, Mam.'

Ciaran was playing with a toy car, oblivious to our conversation.

'Come on,' I nudged him. 'Let's go to school.'

'Can I call for Timmy Higgins?'

'No; now come on then slowcoach, we'd better get going.' He could be so slow when it came to getting ready to go anywhere.

He caught my eye and grinned. 'If you'll buy me a lollipop on the way.'

'OK,' I said. 'Now hurry up.' I'd have given him anything just to get us both out of there.

We left, though Ciaran trailed after me. Maeve joined us and we caught his hand and swung him along the path playing the 'don't walk on the cracks or you'll marry the devil' game. Feeling queasy, I left him in his playground, and Maeve and I continued on to our school. At the gates I made a beeline for the toilets, telling Maeve I'd see her in class.

'Stella. You'll be late for school.' Mam's voice called up the stairs the next morning. 'What's wrong with you?' she asked when I appeared in the kitchen.

I fobbed her off saying it was stomach cramp and sat down.

'Here, eat some breakfast, you'll feel better.'

The look of the congealed egg on toast she put in front of me made my stomach turn. 'No thanks,' I said through clenched teeth. Jumping up I ran to the outside lavatory, my hand over my mouth to stave off the retching. I barely made it to the toilet but managed to turn on the tap so that Mam wouldn't hear me vomiting if she went into the pantry. Afterwards, I locked the door so that Ciaran wouldn't barge in on me, and sat on the toilet seat until the dizziness left me.

'Look at the state of you,' Mam said. 'You'll have to see Doctor Clark if that bug doesn't go.'

Outside the school gates Ciaran wrapped his arms

around me and gave me a bear hug, squeezing my stomach painfully.

'Ouch!' I said, pushing him away.

'You're always in bad humour lately, Stella,' he said, his lower lip quivering.

'No, I'm not.' I ruffled his hair. 'I'll be in good humour this evening, I promise.' He ran in through the gates without looking back at me.

Mary Brown was standing at the wash basins when I came out of the toilet.

'You look terrible. Have you been sick,' she asked.

Mortified, I splashed water on my face. 'I've just got a bug,' I said, washing my hands.

The next morning I had to rush to the toilets in school again.

Mary was again waiting for me when I came out. She gave me a suspicious look. 'Are you sure that it's only a bug?' she asked pointedly, a knowing grin on her face.

'Mind your own business, Mary,' I shouted at her and she reeled back a little, shocked at my aggression.

For the rest of the week Mary paraded in front of me in the schoolyard, her big shoes slapping off the tarmac. She'd stop to dig her friends in the ribs with her elbow and whisper into their ears. I ignored them but my silence caused more curiosity than any nasty retorts. It was awful to go through. I felt like a trapped animal, scared every day as I went into my classroom.

Then one evening sitting on the back wall of Maeve's house, I said to her, 'My monthlys are late.'

'How late?'

'It's been almost six weeks since my last period, and I'm sick every morning.'

She looked at me, turning pale. 'Stella! You're not pregnant, are you?'

'No! I can't be. We only did it once.'

'That's what I thought,' she said, and kept walking, her head down. We sat down on the bench in the schoolyard.

'I feel rotten all the time, I can't stop vomiting.'

'You might have appendicitis,' she said. 'Monica Brady was vomiting all the time before she had hers out.'

I swallowed back my tears. 'Even a taste of tea makes me feel sick, and I can't bear the smell of cooking.'

Maeve said, 'Mam was exactly the same when she was expecting Nuala.'

Panic-stricken, I looked at her. She put her arm around me in an effort to comfort me. 'Did you tell Charles that you were feeling sick?'

'No, I've hardly seen him.' I put my head in my hands. 'Oh God! What am I going to do?'

'You'll have to make an appointment to see Doctor Clark.'

I shook my head. 'I can't face Doctor Clark.'

Maeve had a determined look on her face. 'You've got to, Stella. This is serious. You need to find out if you are pregnant. You can't go on not knowing. I'll come with you.'

But I couldn't bring myself to go to the surgery yet. I decided to go to confession instead, to our new curate Father Moroney.

Goosebumps prickled my skin as I knelt in the dark confession box. I felt light-headed as the shutter went back.

'Bless me, Father, for I have sinned,' I began.

'Yes, my child?'

I looked at the shadowy profile. 'I've done a terrible thing, Father. I can't tell anyone, I'm too frightened.'

'It couldn't be that bad,' he said.

'It is, Father.'

'I'm here to help you, child,' he coaxed and waited.

'I had sex with a boy.'

'I see. Did you go all the way?' The dark and his soothing voice made it easier for me to confess my sin.

'Yes, Father.'

'How many times?'

'Once, Father.'

'That's all?'

'Yes, Father.'

He listened, nodding his head in understanding as I talked, finishing with, 'For these and for all my sins I am sorry and ask God's pardon.'

'For your penance say a decade of the rosary, my child,'

he said, forgiving me and making the sign of the cross. 'Anything else on your mind?'

'I think I'm pregnant, Father, and I don't know what to do.' I held my breath as I waited for his reaction.

After a brief silence he said, 'You must be brave and tell your family.'

'I can't do that, Father. My Mam would kill me.'

'Let me remind you of the love of God, his understanding, and his forgiveness to us who are, after all, only human. Go and tell your mother. It will be all right.' I looked at his dark head through the latticed window and believed him.

I felt as light as air as I knelt before the golden light of the tabernacle and said my penance. It felt as though God himself had come down from heaven and set me free. I was in a state of grace, I was afraid of nothing. All the way home I composed my script for Mam, but when I got there my courage failed me.

A week later I went to see Doctor Clark, sneaking into the surgery in the quiet of the afternoon. There was no one in the waiting room. Doctor Clark greeted me with a hurried smile, and brought me into his office.

'What can I do for you, Stella?' he asked with a quizzical raise of his eyebrows.

'I'm feeling sick all the time, Doctor,' I said nervously.

He smiled gently. 'Don't worry, I'm sure there's nothing seriously wrong,' he said reassuringly. 'Let's just take a look at you.' He took my blood pressure, squinting at the dial, then released it and asked, 'When was your last period?'

'About seven weeks ago.'

'Is that your normal cycle?'

'No, it's usually every four weeks.'

'Have you been sexually active?'

'Yes.'

He tried to hide his shock as he said, 'All right, Stella. I'll have to give you an internal examination.'

I hadn't expected this. Mortified, I went behind a screen and removed my things. While he examined me I concentrated on the view of the sky through the window, praying that I'd got it wrong.

As soon as Doctor Clark had finished he went back to his desk, telling me to get dressed.

'You're pregnant,' he said, his eyes focused and unblinking as I sat down at his desk.

I burst into tears.

'Don't cry. I know that it is a most unfortunate situation to find yourself in at your age, but it's a fact and we'll have to deal with it. Your mother doesn't know, does she?'

'No!'

'She'll have to be told. Because you're so young, you'll need looking after. You're probably a little anaemic, too.' He stood up and came round the desk, turned down my lower eyelids. 'Yes, you'll have to take vitamins and folic acid.'

'I can't tell Mam, she'll go mad,' I sobbed.

'You don't have a choice. You can't get away with keeping your condition a secret from her. You'll have to tell her and the sooner the better. You're going to need her support. It'll be a shock to her but she'll come round. Your young man? Does he know?'

'No.'

'He'll stand by you if he's responsible person,' he said, trying to sound positive. 'Is he in a position to marry you?'

'No.'

'Can he give you financial support?'

'No, he's still at school.' I sniffed.

Doctor Clark reached across and took my hand. 'This is not an illness, Stella. It's a condition. Not the best one to be in, but one I can deal with. Now, dry your eyes. It's not the end of the world,' he said kindly, adding, 'Come and see me in a month. And if you want me to talk to your Mam, I will.'

'Thanks, Doctor.'

Mary Brown was coming out of her shop as I left. I was careful not to catch her eye.

The next afternoon, Maeve and I took the short cut along the lane by the river. Mary Brown, flanked by Peggy Maloney and Sadie O'Sullivan – two girls from our class – came towards us, their faces dark, with the hot sun behind them.

Mary said in an insulting lilt, 'I think Stella has a secret.'

'What is it?' they asked in unison, gathering round me, primed and eager.

The lane was the place where you told secrets. I was always dying to have one but now that I did, I certainly didn't want to confide in them.

'I don't have a secret.' I looked away.

'It's about Charles Thornton, I bet,' Mary snorted.

'That's not a secret,' Sadie said.

'I think he's given her something,' Mary said smugly.

'What?' Peggy asked.

'Tell them,' Mary said, her head tilting, moving forward, ready for the kill.

I took my bracelet out of my blazer pocket, glad I had it to distract them. They examined it, holding it up to the sunlight. The Miraculous Medal charm shone a clear blue so that you could almost see through it.

'It's lovely,' said Peggy begrudgingly, handing it back.

I returned it to my blazer pocket.

'It's a much bigger present than *that*,' Mary taunted.

'Tell us,' Sadie asked.

'It's not fair, we tell you all our secrets,' Peggy lied.

Mary stuck her head forward. 'I saw you coming out of the surgery yesterday, Stella,' she said, looking me straight in the eye.

The others squealed with laughter, except for Maeve, who was furious.

'Stop teasing her,' she shouted at them.

'I know what it is,' Mary said, in a singsong voice.

'You shut up, Mary Brown!' I snapped. 'You don't know anything.' I kicked at a stone, kidding myself that I wasn't scared, and walked on.

But Mary persisted, following Maeve and me down the lane. 'Does your Mam know, Ginger?' she taunted me.

Little jabs of fear shot through me. The smell of damp earth and stagnant water from the shallow river that ran along by the lane made me feel sick. I turned aside and kept my eyes averted to stop the urge to throw up. It didn't work. Clamping my hand over my mouth and went behind the wall and down the ditch. Crouched by the river I vomited, hardly able to believe that this was happening to me in front of them. Wiping my mouth with the back of my hand I sat back on my hunkers, wishing the stream would open up and swallow me. I wanted to escape down into its dark, muddy depths and stay there, for ever hidden, so that they'd never find out my secret.

'She's being sick again,' Mary called out triumphantly, leaning on the wall, looking down at me, laughing.

'It's all your fault,' Maeve said crossly to her. 'Teasing her like that. Now clear off, all of you.'

I dipped my hanky in the water and washed the sick off the front of my white blouse, then slowly made my way back, not wanting to face them again.

They were walking ahead, their voices lowered so we couldn't hear what they were saying.

Maeve nudged me in the ribs. 'Don't take any notice of them, silly fools,' she said, putting her arm around my shoulders. 'Don't let them see that you're upset.'

At the end of the lane Mary turned and gave me a malicious smile. I ignored her and walked on with Maeve, trying to conceal the wet patch on my blouse, and feeling pathetic and alone.

Five

The sickness grew worse and continued each morning followed by a hollow feeling in the pit of my stomach. One morning I was so sick that Mam made me stay in bed. She took a day off work, fussed over me, propped up my pillows, and put a cup of water on the chair beside my bed, warning me with a worried frown not to get up.

I lay there listening to the whirr of her sewing machine and the time signal bleeping out ten o'clock on the radio, and wondered about having a baby. I'd read up on it – even about the actual birth. There was an article in one of Irene's magazines, called *Natural Childbirth*, in which 'labour' was described as 'pain free' if the right breathing techniques were used. It didn't tell me what these 'techniques' were, and I had no way of finding out.

I wondered what would happen to me when Mam found out? I couldn't postpone telling her for much longer. In a few months I would be changing shape, and she'd notice. I loved Mam. I didn't want to hurt her. In tears I turned my head into the pillow, fell asleep, and dreamed of running away to live in a strange town, where no one knew me. There I would have my baby alone. A distraught Charles would finally come to find our baby son and me and bring us home to live happily ever after.

I woke up feeling so lonely that I wanted to die.

Mother Gabriel announced that there would be a one-day silent retreat the week before the summer holidays and that Father Cooney, the parish priest, would be giving it. I dreaded it.

When the day arrived, Father Cooney gave his sermon on sin while Mary Brown sat staring at me, a sly smile playing on her lips. I prayed for forgiveness for the terrible sin I had committed. I asked God to give me the grace to tell Mam and to make her accept the situation. I prayed that Charles would be able to accept and love the baby too. All the time Mary Brown shot me knowing looks, and later she sat huddled in the playground with her pals, whispering. I knew by her face that she was badmouthing me behind my back when she was meant to be reading the lives of the saints. I read the life story of St Therese of Lisieux, and made up my mind to try to imitate her 'Little Way' and offer all my worries and anxieties up to God.

From that day on I pretended Mary didn't exist, except on the last day of school when all of us were saying our goodbyes. Mary gripped my hand and wrung it tightly – sending a searing pain shooting up my arm – a triumphant grin on her face as she did so.

I started working three days a week in the café for the holidays, and decided to tell Charles that I was pregnant as soon as his exams were over. He had a right to know, and with him by my side I was convinced I wouldn't be so scared and alone.

The first Saturday after the exams, Charles was waiting outside the café when I finished work. He was leaning against the railings, his sports bag slung over his shoulder, his jacket stuffed into it.

'Hi,' he said with a smile.

'How did the exams go?' I asked anxiously.

'Not great. The Maths paper was difficult, but I might just scrape through. How are you?'

'I'm OK.' I looked away, unable to meet his eyes.

'You don't seem OK. What's up?' he asked.

'We can't talk here, let's go somewhere quiet,' I said, putting off the moment of telling him, dreading it.

Overcome by a sudden pang of fear, I walked ahead. Charles caught up with me. We didn't speak to one another until we were at the beach, and then Charles put his hand on my arm to detain me. 'What's up, Stella? You're acting very strange.'

'I'm feeling a little sick,' I said.

'Is it serious? What's the matter?' he asked.

'It's . . .' For what seemed ages I couldn't speak, couldn't even breathe. I'd rehearsed what I would say over and over in my head, pictured the scene many times. So why was it so hard to get the words out?

'Come on, tell me,' he said, a note of anxiety in his voice.

But my voice failed me.

'Tell me, Stella.' His voice was urgent now.

Finally I said, 'Can't you guess?' My eyes were on the sky, studying it.

'No.' He looked around him as if he might find the answer in the air.

Shivering with fear, I turned to face him. 'I'm in trouble.' My breath came out in a sob.

He leaned closer. 'What kind of trouble?'

'I'm . . . going to have a baby.' I could barely get the words out.

Startled, he looked at me. 'A baby! This is a joke. You're having me on . . .' He smiled tentatively, waiting for me to laugh.

'Believe me, I wish it *was* a joke,' I shouted over the noise of the waves, my face burning. 'I went to see Doctor Clark. He confirmed it.'

'How far gone are you?'

'About seven weeks.'

Grabbing my arm, he shouted, 'Why didn't you tell me before?'

'I wasn't sure, and I was scared, and you were doing your exams.'

Charles swivelled around to face me fully, blinking at me as though I had betrayed him. 'Are you sure it's mine?' he asked. His words were like a blade, slicing me in two.

'How can you ask that?' I said angrily. 'You know I've never been with anyone else.' A thin line of perspiration shone on his upper lip and he turned away, but I grabbed his arm and forced him to look at me. 'You know I haven't.'

A look of fear and realisation spread over Charles's face as he fixed his eyes on me. They were dark and deep, the eyes of a stranger. I bit my lip, fighting to keep back the tears. 'I'm telling you the truth. You know I am. You're just scared, that's all.'

He stood staring out at the hazy horizon. He believed me at last.

'I've got to go. I've got to think.' He raked his hand through his hair, twisted away, and began to walk across the beach.

'Charles, wait!' I jumped up, scrambled after him, my shoes sinking deeper and deeper into the sand with every step, until I was standing behind him.

He turned. We almost collided.

'It isn't fair to blame it all on me.' Though I was blaming myself as much. Nothing I could do would ever be as bad or as stupid as getting pregnant, as far as he was concerned. 'Charles, say something, please,' I begged.

He ducked out of reach. 'We'll talk about it later when we've both cooled off,' he said, and began to walk away.

'Don't go.' My pathetic plea was lost in the wind.

Charles turned back for a moment, raised his shoulders in a shrug, then continued on walking.

I stood in a daze staring after him, watching his back recede until he was out of sight. Then I sat down on the sand and listened to the waves break and roar in the distance, the sun on my face. I ran the sand through my fingers, picked up a handful of smooth, round pebbles and played with them as the waves thundered to the shore. I wished I could forget everything: who I was, where I came from, my family. Most of all I wished I could forget the strange, cold Charles. The sun beat down; the pebbles lay in my fingers like loyal friends. I lay back, holding them. They warmed my hands.

The water lapping at my feet stirred me from my thoughts and forced me to move. The sun had gone in and it was starting to rain. Rising slowly, my sodden feet sinking into the wet sand, I made my way back up the beach. Shivering, I walked home numb as a sleepwalker. I took the short cut across the fields. Mam would be wondering where I'd been. I resolved to be brave and tell her everything and face the consequences, but my mind felt numb and my feet and legs were stiff with the cold as I let myself in.

Mam was washing up in the kitchen. She looked haggard. 'Where were you?' She asked.

I cleared my throat. 'Walking.' I took off my shoes.

'In the sea I'd say, by the cut of you.' I thought she was going to rant at me but all she said was, 'You missed your tea.'

'I'm not hungry.'

'It's daft to be out walking on the beach on your own this hour of the evening when there's nobody about.'

I didn't answer.

'You are not to do it again. You hear me?'

'Yes. Goodnight, Mam.'

I washed my feet, got into bed, drew my knees up to my chin and lay there drained of all feeling, listening to the rain bouncing off the slate roof, thinking of Charles's shocked reaction to my news. I'd never be able to face him again now. I began to plan my escape. I would take my savings of twenty pounds out of the post office and pretend I was going shopping. I would get the bus to Dublin, then take the boat to Holyhead. The only trouble was that I didn't know what Dad's address was because he kept moving from place to place.

In the morning the pale sunshine streamed through the window, waking me up. I heard the sound of Mam's footsteps in the kitchen and the kettle whistling on the stove. Suddenly, the memory of the previous evening flooded in. I lay watching dust motes dance in the light, wondering what on earth I was going to do.

Mam came into my room with a mug of tea. 'Thought

you might like a hot cuppa to wake you up.' I watched her quick fingers pulling back the curtains.

'Thanks, Mam.' I sat up, took a sip of tea.

Half an hour later I was dressed and in the kitchen. Rashers sizzled in the frying pan. I took one just to please Mam, but couldn't eat it. Ciaran was daydreaming over his porridge.

'Come on, son,' Mam coaxed. 'Eat up or you'll be late for mass.'

Groaning, Ciaran flung himself down off his chair. Eventually, Mam got him ready and the three of us went to mass as usual.

I could barely concentrate on the service, and when we came out of the church Charles was waiting for me outside the gates. I went over to him. 'Stella,' he said. 'I'm sorry for all those awful things I said to you.' He looked contrite and he'd certainly calmed down, but looking into his eyes I saw that a barrier had gone up between us. 'Meet me at the beach at three o'clock,' he said and turned away to the street. 'I'll be waiting.'

On the way to the beach a mental image of us flashed in front of my eyes. We were walking along like a family, Charles happily laughing as he tumbled our baby son in the air.

He was waiting for me at our usual place. I longed for him to put his arm around me, tell me that everything would be all right. Instead he said, pointedly, 'What are you going to do?'

'I don't know,' I said truthfully.

'Have you told your mother?'

I shook my head. 'I'm too frightened to tell her. She doesn't suspect anything either because the idea of sex outside of marriage is unthinkable to her. I do know that when she finds out she'll kill me.'

'And send for this big, bad wolf,' he said, pointing to himself, his eyes full of resentment.

'Possibly.'

'Bridie had a baby once,' he said reflectively.

'What happened to it?' I asked in surprise.

'She got rid of it. My mother helped her.'

I suddenly felt very cold. My stomach clenched in a knot as I looked at him. 'And you think I should do the same?'

'It would solve a lot of problems. I could find out from Bridie how to go about it.'

Instinctively I put my hands over my stomach. 'I'm not going to have an abortion,' I said calmly.

'Other girls do it.'

'I'm not like other girls.' I said, anger flaring up inside me. 'It's nothing to you, I know, just a stupid mistake. To me it's a baby, a life growing inside me.'

A look of fear and horror spread over his face. 'Stella, listen to me.' He reached out to me.

'No. Don't touch me!' I shouted at him. 'I don't have to listen to you and I don't have to do what you tell me to. I pushed past him and ran down the beach. It was all going horribly wrong again.

'Stella!' Charles caught up with me, grabbed my arm. 'I'm sorry. Please, listen,' he pleaded.

'No. You're ashamed of me, you don't want to have anything to do with me, or with the baby.' I was crying now.

Charles leaned forward; he put his head down in despair. 'It's not that. I just don't know what else to do.'

'Neither do I. It's awful to go through, worse than anything I'd ever imagined, but I can't kill my own flesh and blood.' I breathed in to stop more tears from coming.

'Listen, we'll work this out,' he said.

'How?'

He was examining his hands as though looking for a solution of our situation in them. 'I'll get a job,' he said, resignation in his ashen face. The lads are going to England to work for the summer on building sites. I'm going with them. They've arranged accommodation and all that. I'll save, get a flat, you can come over in a month or two and have the baby there. No one need ever know.'

'But you don't want this baby.' I was crying.

'No, but we'll manage. Now stop crying, sweetheart,' he said in a falsely cheerful voice.

I softened when he called me 'sweetheart,' as I always did, and smiled through my tears. He promised that we would be strong for one another and keep our secret until I was safely in England.

'That's my girl, we'll get through this,' he said, looking uncomfortable. I knew that things would not work out that simply but still I forced a smile on my face, too scared to question him further for the moment.

At the corner of our street Charles said goodbye, promising to write as soon as he arrived in London. In that split second, when I looked into his eyes, I wondered if he ever would.

Six

Mam and Mrs Ruane were sipping tea when I got in from the café the next evening. Mam was holding a letter up to the light as if it was an X-ray she was trying to see through.

'Is that from Dad?'

'Yes, he says he's changing jobs and he hopes to send more money soon. He doesn't seem to miss us, though,' she said in a dull voice, scrutinising the letter as if for some hidden evidence. 'I never dreamed a scrap of paper would be my only contact with my husband.'

'Maybe he's made new friends,' I said. 'You don't want him to be lonely over there, do you?'

Mrs Ruane said sensibly, 'Luckily you've plenty to keep you busy, what with rearing these two and your little job.'

'Yes, but I'm owed for two frocks I made for a new customer, and I owe Mrs Brown for the material, and not a sign of getting paid,' Mam said.

'Which means you're working for nothing,' Mrs Ruane supplied.

'Exactly.'

Rolling up her sleeves, Mrs Ruane said, 'Give me the name and address of that customer and I'll go round and give her a warning to pay up or else.' Mrs Ruane liked nothing better than a good fight.

'Thanks, but I'll leave it for a bit longer if you don't mind. I have a few pounds put by to see me through next week.' Mam paused, stirred her tea.

'I'll do an extra day at the café, Mam,' I said.

'That'll be a help, thanks, love.'

I said goodnight and went to bed. Things were going from bad to worse, I thought as I tried to sleep, but I still tried to convince myself that my hunch about Charles not keeping his word had been wrong.

I functioned, got through each day trying not to think about Charles, but he kept coming into my thoughts anyway. I'd picture him in a crowded pub gazing into his glass, missing me, or walking through strange, deserted streets wishing I were there with him. I even imagined a letter from him telling me to get on the next boat to Holyhead. At night I'd dream about him; see his face clearly, smell the brylcream on his hair, taste his lips on my lips, feel the way his skin felt against my skin. I'd reach out to touch him and would wake up touching the air.

He wrote me a cheerful letter, full of talk of building sites and his 'mates'. The postmark said 'Hackney'. I wrote back and told him that I was coping well and not as sick as I had been. He wrote twice more: short, cheerful letters. Then the letters stopped.

Leaving the café one night, I bumped into Leo.

'Have you heard from Charles?' I asked anxiously.

Leo looked uncomfortable. 'No, but his mother says he's left London and gone off somewhere,' he said.

'What'd you mean, gone off somewhere?'

'Vanished, vamoosed. Nobody seems to know where he is.'

Dumbfounded, I stared at Leo. He couldn't just disappear like that!'

'He has.'

I bit my lip. 'Maybe something's happened to him? Supposing he's come to some harm?' My voice shook.

Leo shook his head. 'His da thinks he's gone to the States.'

'What? Why would he do that?'

'I don't know. Could be because his da's putting pressure on him to come back in case he may have to repeat his exams to get a place in college. He was dead against him going to London in the first place. But Charles doesn't want to come back it seems to me. Ever . . . Are you all right, Stella?'

'Yes, fine.'

'Come on, I'll walk you home.'

'No thanks, I'm all right. If you hear anything, let me know.'

' 'Course I will.'

I watched him until he was out of sight, then burst into tears. For the first time in my life I was really frightened. Charles had deserted me when I needed him most; just when he'd convinced me that we'd have come through things together. Walking home slowly, I realised that the rest of my journey I would have to take alone.

Time went on and there was still no word of Charles. I started to get worried. What if he'd fallen off some scaffolding or off a roof? He could be killed and nobody would know. I wondered what was going through the minds of his mam and dad, not knowing where he was. I wondered if I should call and see them, see how they were. But realising it would be for my own ends that I would be doing this I dismissed the idea.

At the café Irene noticed my anxiety. 'Not heard from Charles yet?' she asked one day.

Just the mention of his name brought him back so vividly that I had to look away to stop myself from crying.

'He seems to have vanished off the face of the earth,' I told her.

'He must have gone for a reason. They're a strange family.' Irene's tone softened as she said, 'Last thing you want is Charles Thornton for a boyfriend, he's from such a different background to ours.'

Later, Maeve said, 'He's treated you badly. I wish you'd picked Leo to fall for, he's much more your type.'

'Leo's a good pal but I'm not interested in him like that,' I said.

'A lot of girls think he's very good looking, and he's really kind too,' Maeve said wistfully.

It was true. And Leo was tall, with broad shoulders, blonde hair, and steady blue eyes. I'd known him for so long that he was like an older brother to me. We'd climbed the trees behind the station together, and he'd tried to teach me how to smoke, rubbing my back afterwards when I'd nearly choked.

Maeve was eyeing me. 'Life not fun any more?'

'How can it be?' I asked. I looked down at my stomach.

'You need something to take your mind off all your problems. What about this party on Saturday night at Stephen's? Stephen likes you and it'll be good fun. Say you'll come,' she coaxed. Stephen is Maeve's cousin.

'In this state?'

'So what? No one will know,' she said, and she had a point.

'OK, I'll come,' I said. What harm could it do after all?

Stephen's house was already crowded when we arrived. Maeve escorted me into the kitchen. Stephen, a tall, attractive boy, was delighted to see us. 'Great to see you, Stella,' he said, smiling at me. I smiled back, determined to appear completely normal. A few of the boys looked me up and down, and I looked back at them, trying to give the impression that I was playing the game too, enjoying myself. Stephen kept glancing at me and when the music started he came over. 'Like to dance?' he asked, raising an eyebrow and making me laugh.

'Why not?' I said, and let him put his arm around me and lead me into the sitting room where the dancing was. We danced to 'It Doesn't Matter Any More,' then when Elvis Presley sang 'A Fool Such As I', Stephen pulled me close, and holding me tightly in his arms breathed heavily into my ear as we moved. The more I tried to get Charles out of my head, the more he stayed. Suddenly, I pulled away.

'What's up?' Stephen murmured, looking at me anxiously.

'Nothing, it's a bit hot in here, that's all.'

'Let's go outside for a breath of fresh air.' He steered me through the back to the door.

Outside I breathed a sigh of relief, feeling better. I sat on the low garden wall with Stephen beside me. He leaned forward and kissed me on the lips suddenly and with such force that I was taken completely by surprise. I pushed him away. 'Sorry, I can't . . .' I began.

'Sorry, I . . .' He looked hurt. But everything about him was wrong: his touch, his smell, and his taste.

'I'm sorry.' I repeated, taking a deep breath. 'I don't feel very well, that's all.'

'Oh!' He looked concerned. 'Do you want me to get you a glass of water?'

'Yes, please.'

Stephen escorted me back into the kitchen and got me a glass of water.

'Thanks,' I said and drank the water, almost choking on it trying not to gag. Excusing myself, I went to the outside lavatory and shot the bolt across the door. I stood, heart pounding, wondering what to do, praying Stephen wouldn't be waiting for me when I came out. I didn't want to hurt his feelings; it wasn't his fault that he wasn't Charles. When I finally did sneak out, the back door was wide open and Bobby Darin's 'Dream Lover' flowed out, filling the air, making me want to cry. The thought of going back in to face the party and Stephen again, and trying to bluster my way through the night, was unbearable. I saw the open gate, the empty road, and the instinct to escape was so strong that I took to my heels and ran as fast as I could.

Near home I slowed down, tottering in my high heels, my feet aching. What would they think when they missed me? Maeve would kill me! I'd have to think of a good excuse so as not to hurt her feelings.

At home, I ran to the bathroom. Brushing my teeth, I felt sick again. Gripping the hand basin, I bent my knees and slowly squatted down, pressing my hands into the walls of my stomach, willing the sick feeling to go away.

'Stella?' Mam called, coming out from her bedroom five minutes later, as I ducked into my bedroom. She followed me inside, staring through me, the sleepiness suddenly gone from her eyes. 'You didn't drink alcohol, did you?' she asked.

'No, of course not. I probably had too much Coca Cola. I'm going to have a bath.'

'A bath? But you had one before you went out. What have you been up to? Look at the state of your shoes!'

'We walked home through the fields,' I lied, feeling like a criminal under her glare.

Next morning I went to apologise to Maeve for running off. She was sulking. 'I thought you were getting on well with Stephen. You seemed to be enjoying yourself, and then whoosh you were gone. You frightened us, disappearing like that. It ruined the night.'

'I was sick,' I said meekly.

'Stella, you'd better tell your Mam about 'you know what' before someone else does,' she advised.

'I will, soon, I promise,' I said, wondering where I was going to find the strength to do it.

I carried on playing a part, pretending to get on with my life, and continued to work at the café – which was a real effort because the smell of fried food and coffee made me feel sick. But I acted the part so well it seemed that I fooled everyone.

Irene said, one morning out of the blue, 'You're getting over Charles all the same.'

'Yes, I suppose so,' I said, cleaning the coffee machine. I couldn't tell her that I wasn't over him at all. That I thought about him all the time. I kept Charles's photo in my top drawer. I put his bracelet on each night and took it off in the morning. I felt half alive, going through the motions but secretly reliving our time together, gazing at his photograph – talking to it, even – keeping him alive in my little fantasy world, so that he was more real to me than what was happening in my life. I spent all of my time imagining us being together. But it didn't lessen the continuous knot of pain in the pit of my stomach that wouldn't go away, no matter how hard I tried to get rid of it.

One day I saw Mr Thornton getting out of his big car in the town. A stern-looking man with broad shoulders, he walked purposefully towards his office. Then, late one afternoon, I bravely walked past Charles's house in the faint hope that he might have returned home and I hadn't heard. Mrs Thornton was in the garden tending her flowerbeds methodically. She didn't look like a woman whose son had disappeared. I wondered if she was thinking about Charles. She looked so calm that it was impossible to know. I tried to imagine what would she say if she knew about my pregnancy? The thought of a little son or daughter of Charles's running around her beautiful garden, messing up her flowerbeds, was probably unimaginable to her.

Several times after that I would find myself passing Charles's house in the vain hope of seeing him. Once I hid behind a tree thinking he might appear. I needed help, and I knew it. Maeve was the only one who knew my condition, and she was sworn to secrecy. I had managed to deceive most people, but I knew that I couldn't keep up the pretence for much longer because I was feeling sicker than ever and losing weight.

Seven

The extra day's work at Irene's was exhausting. In the mornings I felt so tired that I was hardly able to get out of bed.

One time Mam heard me retching. 'Stella, are you sick again?' she asked.

'Something I ate,' I said, swaying on my feet.

'It can't be the food in the café that's doing this to you,' she muttered. 'If it was, all the customers would be getting sick and Irene would have the health inspectors in.'

Ciaran said, 'You might have caught an incurable disease, like leprosy.'

'Ciaran, don't talk daft,' Mam said to him.

'We're learning leprosy in Religion. Sister Mary said that bits of you fall off.'

'There's no such thing as leprosy in this country.' Mam threw her eyes to heaven, and decided to send Ciaran to the surgery to ask Doctor Clark to call in on me on his way home. I begged her not to but she wouldn't listen. She made me go back to bed.

When I heard the sound of Doctor Clark's care outside

my window and his footstep on the path, I lay face-down into my pillow dreading the knock on the door.

'She's not eating, and the little she does eat she can't keep down,' I heard Mam say to him.

Doctor Clark came into the room.

'Stella,' he said in a loud, cheerful voice, and stood towering over my bed.

'Hello Doctor,' I said, mortified.

He sat at the side of the bed, examined my tummy. In a hushed voice he said, 'You didn't tell her?'

His face swam before me. 'No, Doctor, I didn't.'

'She has to be told, you know that.'

I nodded. He opened the door and called Mam in.

'Mrs Wood, Stella is pregnant,' he said gently.

'What!' Mam's mouth opened wide in amazement. 'She can't be,' she choked. 'You must have it wrong.'

He shook his head, 'Sadly, I'm afraid I haven't,' he said.

'But she hasn't been . . . with anyone. Sure she's only a child herself, Doctor,' Mam cried, looking from me to him in disbelief.

'Well . . . these things happen, Mrs Wood. We've got to concentrate on looking after Stella now, we don't want anything to go amiss, do we?' Doctor Clark said, sitting on the side of the bed, opening his bag and taking out his blood pressure machine. Mam stood with her hands to her mouth, probably trying to stop a scream escaping from her lips.

'Your blood pressure is perfect,' Doctor Clark said,

putting away his machine, snapping his bag shut. Turning to me he said, 'I'll leave you a prescription for folic acid and come and see me in a month's time,' and left, Mam following him out the door like a sleepwalker.

I could hear their voices, Mam saying, 'But a pregnancy out of wedlock, and she not yet sixteen. It is the worst thing that could befall us, Doctor.'

Doctor Clark said, 'I know, this is not an easy situation. Stella has been foolish. Now you must be strong and help her.' His words faded out as they went outside together, and I heard the click of the door.

From the window I saw them talking together, Doctor Clark's mouth making strange shapes, Mam grimacing, then wiping her eyes as he stepped into his car. When he finally pulled away from the kerb I waited, petrified for her return.

When she came inside, Mam stood still for a moment looking at me, her face twitching in anger. Then she gripped my arm, dragged me out of bed, and marched me into the kitchen, roaring as she went, 'Whose baby is it? Is it that Charles Thornton? Is he the father?' Even the fridge trembled in her wake.

I nodded, too terrified to speak.

'How could you!' she shrieked. 'You stupid, stupid girl.'

'I'm sorry, Mam.' I choked.

She slammed her fist on the table. 'Sorry isn't good enough. You've been coming and going, telling me lies about where it is you're spending your time. To think I didn't see what was going on under my nose.' Breathing hard, her mouth an angry hard slit, she came after me and hit me smartly across the face. My knees buckled. 'You're no better than the rest of those loose girls that hang around the town. You think Charles Thornton will stand by you? Well, let me tell you he won't.' She was madder than I'd ever seen her, choking her words out. 'You think he loves you? Well, he doesn't. He's using you, that's what he's doing!' The room swirled around me as her arm swung out and grabbed me again. 'You lying, deceitful, dirty little slut,' she shouted.

'Leave her alone.' Ciaran's voice was faint in the distance. 'Mam, leave her alone,' he screamed.

'Mam, please!' I bit my lip, tasted salt on my tongue. My mouth opened and closed but the words that came out sounded fuzzy.

'He'll drop you when he finds out that you're pregnant. Mark my words.'

I swerved past her, and made for the bedroom door and locked it. I dressed quickly, opened my window wide, then climbed out, and soon I was running across the embankment. I sprinted along, not stopping until I reached the beach and a dark corner where I could hide. There, I sank into the soft wet sand, my head spinning, and Mam's voice ringing in my ears, the terrible names she'd called me still bouncing around in my head. I covered my ears to stop them and stared out at the horizon.

The world was falling apart. I pushed myself back against our boulder, and stared at the dim line of the sea and the red glow of the sun sinking into the horizon until it disappeared, wishing I could disappear like Charles had done.

I stayed there, numb, until the cold water lapping my feet made me shiver. It was dark; a full moon lit the sky and cast shadows on the road as I walked slowly back home. As I sneaked in I strained my ears for the sound of the radio, hoping against hope that Mam had gone to bed, scared to face her again. But I heard nothing except the sound of Ciaran lightly snoring.

When I came into the kitchen next morning Mam was getting breakfast, slamming drawers and cupboards. My stomach churned.

'I thought that you were a good normal, happy, Catholic girl getting on well, and now suddenly you're something else,' she said immediately, obviously still furious with me.

I kept my eyes on the swirls of the linoleum floor as I drank my tea, picturing myself with a halo hovering over my head, a chorus of angels sitting on white clouds above my head.

'How am I going to tell your dad? It would kill him if he found out that his innocent little girl had turned into a . . .' She began to cry.

'What, Mam?' Ciaran asked, coming into the kitchen, sprawling himself across a chair. 'What has Stella turned into?' He looked from one of us to the other, bewildered.

'A monster, apparently,' I said to stop his questions.

Mam sat down with her cup of tea, tears spilling down her cheeks. Ciaran sat in silence, looking frightened. After a minute or so Mam cleared her throat and dried her eyes, but she wouldn't look at him. Eventually he gave up and went out to the back garden to play.

For ages afterwards Mam sat gazing out through the window, the smoke from her cigarette twisting into the air, her sleeves rolled up to her elbows, ready to start on her sewing. But she didn't move. She didn't go to work, she stopped sewing at home, and stayed in bed for two days, staring out at the sky all day, only getting up to make herself a cup of tea.

On the mornings when she didn't get up Ciaran trailed around, his head drooping. I stayed with him, did the shopping, made his dinner: fried eggs and chips, ham and potatoes. Mam wouldn't eat a thing. Mrs Ruane came and went. I could hear them whispering together in Mam's bedroom. One day Mrs Ruane said to me, 'You mother needs to see a doctor, she very depressed,' her eyes on me accusingly like drawn daggers.

I sent Ciaran for Doctor Clark. He said that Mam was suffering from nervous exhaustion – she was in danger of becoming seriously ill if the whole family didn't pull its weight and help her.

'What whole family are you talking about?' Mam said. 'Sure there's only Stella and Ciaran.'

'I think your husband should be told of these new circumstances,' he said, casting a glance towards me.

'No.' Mam was emphatic. 'He'd only come home, and we need the money too badly for him to be out of work.'

Doctor Clark gave her a prescription for antidepressants and left, reminding me to call in for a check up soon.

When Mam finally did get up and get dressed she sat at the kitchen table all morning staring into space and smoking. She only spoke to issue instructions: do this . . . get that . . . She didn't even listen to the radio.

'Why is Mam always crying?' Ciaran asked, later in the afternoon. He was playing with his cars.

'She's lonely.'

'But she has you and me. And why are you sick all the time?' he asked, lining up his cars on the cardboard racetrack I'd made for him.

'I'm not.'

'Yes, you are. I heard you and Maeve whispering in the dark the other night about you being sick all the time.'

'You shouldn't be listening to grown-up conversations, you bold boy.'

'You're not a grown-up.'

I swiped at his arm playfully.

'Ouch!' I'm telling on you.' He ducked his head and ran off shouting, 'Stella hit me.'

I grabbed him, pulled him back. 'Shh – you'll only make things worse.'

Mam was at work on a dress for a customer. She stopped at our squabble and looked at me over the bar of her sewing machine, as if she was looking down at me through the barrel of a rifle.

One afternoon I took Ciaran to the beach to give Mam a break. We went to Byrne's sweet shop on the way.

'What would you like?' Mrs Byrne asked him.

'Don't know.' He drooled over the jars of honeybees and peg's legs and aniseed balls, Cleeve's toffees and penny chews on the counter, taking his time.

'How's your Mam? Mrs Byrne asked me. 'I haven't seen her lately. Is she all right?'

'She cries all the time,' Ciaran said.

'Is that so?' Mrs Byrne said, leaning her big arms on the counter, looking me straight in the eye as she settled in for a good gossip. 'Is she sick then?'

I wanted to say, 'Mind your own business,' but I didn't have the nerve.

Ciaran did. 'Yes she is,' he said. 'Very sick!'

'Oh! What ails her?' Mrs Byrne asked me.

'She misses Dad,' Ciaran said, before I had a chance to reply.

'Sure your da'll be back for a holiday before you know it, and in the meantime he's sending money home, isn't he?'

I nudged Ciaran with my elbow. 'Whayawant?' I said under my breath, gesturing at the sweets on display.

Ciaran couldn't make up his mind. He was busy thinking up some other story to get Mrs Byrne's sympathy and extra free sweets. In the end I made him choose and practically dragged him out of the shop.

'Come on, Ciaran.' I tugged at his sleeve. 'We're off to the beach,' I said to Mrs Byrne.

'Tell your ma I was asking for her,' she said, wrapping in a paper cone the ten honeybees he'd picked for a penny and giving him a free gobstopper on the way out, and patting him on the head.

'Whatdasay?' I elbowed him again.

'Thanks, Mrs Byrne.' His smile dimpled his face as he licked the green goo.

'Pity she didn't give it to you on the way in,' I said, giving him a shove. 'You shouldn't be telling our business to people.'

'She asked me!' he protested, licking like mad.

At the beach we combed among the pebbles for shells to add to his collection. We found blue ones, silvery ones, and brown ones speckled with russet. Ciaran washed each one carefully in the sea, counting them into his empty sweet bag as he did so. A man with a terrier walked by. Ciaran chased the dog around, whooping like a cowboy out of a green, sticky mouth, sending the dog into a frenzy of delight. At the edge of the sea I grabbed him and washed his face while he squirmed away, jumping in and out of the rolling waves, then digging his toes in the sand making footprints for the tide to wash away. Watching him, I longed to be a child again. Life would be a lot easier.

The sun was low behind the trees as we walked home, turning them into dark, eerie shapes. Ciaran was scared. To distract him I got him to pick out the stars as they began to appear in the sky like Dad used to do; his hand tucked safely into mine. He named Orion's Belt, the Big Dipper, and the Northern Star.

'I miss Dad,' Ciaran said, gazing up at them.

'So do I,' I said, and meant it with all my heart.

'Has he forgotten us, do you think?' he asked.

'No, of course not. How could he when he loves us so much.'

Satisfied, his step lightened.

Eight

Father's Cooney's Morris Minor was parked outside our house one evening when I got home. I sneaked in. Outside the kitchen door I could hear Mam's voice, hushed and urgent as she said, 'Under my very eyes and I knew nothing about it, Father. I don't know how she could do such a thing.' Her voice was odd, almost unrecognisable.

'Unbelievable, Eileen. It's a disgrace. That it should happen to a God-fearing woman like yourself,' came Father Cooney's deep-toned reply.

'She's not yet sixteen.' Her voice rose with disbelief.

'So young,' came the reply. 'She's big for her age, and far too beautiful for her own good. She doesn't understand the wicked ways of this modern world. Young people behave differently nowadays. Teenagers, that's what they call themselves,' he said.

'I don't care what they call themselves, they're nothing but trouble. I hope you know that nothing like this ever happened before in my family, Father.'

'Who's the boy involved?'

'Charles Thornton.'

'But they're *Protestants*.' Father Cooney's voice rose for the first time.

'I know, I've made it clear to her that nothing can come of it. He won't want anything to do with her.'

'Does he know about this?'

'He's gone off to England with the lads, working and having a good time. Between you and me, Father, I don't think she'll be seeing him again, and here I am without her father to help me.' The anxiety in Mam's voice made it crackle.

' 'Tis a terrible state of affairs. Something will have to be done, Eileen.'

Mam burst into tears. In a gasping breath she said, 'But I don't know what to do. I can't cope on my own, Father.'

'You'll have to get her away from here.' Father Cooney cleared his throat. 'Trust in God, Eileen; we'll think of something.' His tone was hushed and comforting now.

A cold lump of fear formed deep inside of me. My stomach clenched as I opened the door. They were sipping tea together, one of the best blue willow-pattern plates between them full of home-made queen cakes. They stopped talking abruptly when they saw me.

'Stella! Hello there.' Tall and gangling, Father Cooney got to his feet awkwardly, his face flushing with embarrassment at the sight of me.

I didn't look him in the eye.

'You took your time getting home.' Mam had her martyr face on.

'We walked slowly.'

'Weren't you right,' Father Cooney said, sitting down, his blue-veined hands clasped together as if he was in prayer.

'I'll make another pot of tea.' Mam mopped her eyes and shuffled off.

As soon as she was gone, Father Cooney said, 'Your mother told me your . . . predicament.' His gaze slid down the length of my body and came to rest on the silver buckle of my belt. I pressed into the corner until I could feel the wooden slats of the wainscoting through my frock. 'Sit down, Stella,' he said, swiping back his thin strands of hair with nicotine-stained fingers.

I sat down. Father Cooney coughed to drown out the awful silence, and twiddled his thumbs. I shifted in my chair. The shadows lengthened across the room, deepening the cream walls. I looked into their murky depths, not knowing where else to look.

'Don't be afraid, I won't bite you.' Father Cooney coughed again.

I looked up. He was watching me with his dark eyes. He leaned toward me, shoulders hunched. 'So Stella, I'm going to find you a place to go so that you can have your baby without the world and his wife knowing. That's good, isn't it?' He smiled tensely. I didn't know what he was talking about.

Mam returned with the teapot and refilled the cups. Slowly, Father Cooney stirred his tea, tapping his teaspoon on the saucer. 'I know a convent in Dublin,' he said.

'Convent!' I said, aghast.

He raised his hand. 'It's highly thought of. It's like a school, except that you live in.'

'A boarding school?' I asked.

'Kind of. You'll be living with the nuns; the only difference is that you'll be learning skills instead of book learning.' He smiled. 'You'll be fitted out for life. Lots of girls who get into . . . well, girls like you, have gone there in the past and are very happy.'

I turned to Mam. 'Mam, please don't send me away,' I said to her.

'I don't like the idea one little bit, but you'll have to be looked after somewhere, and it sounds ideal,' she said.

'But it's so far away.'

'Stella, you've done a dreadful thing, now you must take the consequences,' Mam said icily.

'That's right,' Father Cooney sighed.

Sitting there crouched into the chair, my eyes downcast, I remembered Charles's promise to send for me. I had kept repeating it over and over in my head and I did so again now. Anything to help me stop hearing what they were saying to me.

I nearly jumped out of my skin when Father Cooney slapped down his cup and, straightening up, said, 'I'd better be off but don't worry, we'll settle it, Eileen.' He strode out, Mam in his wake, shutting the door behind her.

'Goodbye, Father,' I said under my breath, glad to see him go.

In my bedroom I looked in the mirror, trying to see the beauty Father Cooney had been talking about. The crimson sun burned through the window setting my coppery hair ablaze. It flamed like a fireball, electrifying my eyes and paling my face to a delicate white, making the horrible sprinkling of pink freckles across the bridge of my nose stand out. My mouth was too wide, my cheekbones too high and lately taut with tension. I looked a fright. Father Cooney was right about one thing though: I was big for my age. I looked young and old all at once. I was a freak!

I turned to the window again, willing Charles to come roaring up the road on his motorbike and whisk me off to England where we would live for ever. I closed my eyes and made a wish.

'Father Cooney is a saint,' Mam exclaimed later at tea time. 'Always there when you need him, a godsend in a crisis, takes on the whole burden.'

Next morning I heard drawers opening and shutting in my room. I looked in. Mam was sorting through my clothes with quick, jerky movements, her old, battered suitcase on the floor beside her.

'There isn't much here that still fits you,' she said in a shrill voice as she checked the pile on the floor. 'This might stretch,' she said, 'and that,' she muttered, lifting up a couple of jumpers, discarding others.

I could see that she was close to tears as she started packing. 'This bloody suitcase is useless. Dad's got the good, big one in England. Trust him to be missing all this.' She stopped, bowed her head. 'Oh, you stupid girl, how could you have done this to me?' She banged the suitcase down hard on the floor. 'You get on with it,' she said and marched out of the room.

Ciaran came in. 'Where are you going, Stella?' he asked, a puzzled look on his face.

'I have to go away for a little while,' I said, almost in tears.

'Is it to a hospital? Are you still sick?' he asked, his voice wobbly.

'Sort of. It is a special place where they make you better.'

'But I don't want you to go,' he said.

'I'll be back before you know it,' I lied.

Mam had simmered down when I went into the kitchen. 'It's not easy for me either,' she said.

'I know, Mam.' I went out of the back door so that she and Ciaran wouldn't see me crying.

Maeve was waiting for me, sitting on the wall. 'I heard your Mam shouting. Are you all right?' she asked.

She can't wait to get rid of me before the whole parish finds out, not that I blame her. Father Cooney's arranging to have me sent away.'

'God! Where to?'

'A convent in Dublin. Maeve, I don't want to live in a big convent with a load of awful nuns.' I took a deep breath. 'And Charles is to blame too, and he isn't even here for me. I don't want to go.' Big tears dropped down my face.

She held my arm, shook it gently. 'Tell them that.'

'There's no point, they won't listen.'

'Write to your dad, ask him to come home. He'll come.'

'I don't have his address.'

'I didn't know that. God, Stella, I'm really sorry.'

I sobbed. Her hand reached for mine. 'Listen, I'll write to you every day.'

'I'll write back.' I wanted to explain more about the place I was going to, but a kind of shame prevented me, and I didn't know that much anyway.

'I'll miss you. I'll come and see you with your mam,' she said.

'I don't think Mam'll be coming to see me.' My throat closed over. I couldn't speak.

'I'll think of something.'

That night I sat on my bed, looking out at the stars, wondering how I'd cope without Maeve. I couldn't imagine what life would be like not seeing her every day. We'd been friends all our lives, spent all our spare time in each other's houses, except for the occasional day we didn't speak after some silly row, which was quickly made up. We'd stuck by one another through thick and thin.

No one could have felt lonelier than I did at that moment, with the big black sky above me, and the dark fields and hills around me and a great empty feeling in the pit of my stomach. I loved Knocknacree. I would miss it. I would miss Mam and Ciaran and our house. Wherever I was going I knew there would be no taste like the taste of Mam's cooking. How could I have ruined my life in such a short space of time I wondered? Up until now I'd been a good, loyal daughter who helped Mam as much as I could. I knew where the answer lay. It was Charles Thornton.

Nine

'Stella! Are you ready? We don't want to keep Father Cooney waiting.' Mam had her good black coat on, the sparkly brooch Dad had sent her for her birthday on the lapel, and her silk headscarf with the hunting scene on was tied around her neck. She constantly flitted to the window, looking out every five minutes, her hands fidgety on the net curtains.

Ciaran said, 'Mam, can I come with you?'

She said, 'No, I told you already that Mrs Ruane is taking you to the pictures. John Wayne – Cowboys and Indians, you'll love it,' she said.

'But I want to go with you and Stella,' he whined.

I went back to the bedroom and sat on the bed, wishing there were somewhere I could hide where they would never find me. Ciaran followed me. 'I don't want you to go, Stella,' he whimpered.

'I have to.'

'But why?'

I put my arms around him. 'Because I've done something wrong and now I have to pay for it.'

He looked at me searchingly. 'Is it a lot of money? I've got two pounds in my moneybox.'

'No, love, it's not that kind of payment.'

He began to cry. I pulled him to me, hugged his little body tightly. 'Don't cry,' I soothed. I tried to say I'd write to him often but my voice failed me. I gave him a lollipop I'd been saving for this moment, to distract him. He gave me Bugs, his little floppy rabbit that he slept with, insisting that I take it. Tearfully, I crammed it into the suitcase.

Mam came into the room. 'That suitcase won't shut. How many times have I showed you how to fold everything neatly?' she said, getting down on her hunkers, rearranging the clothes, her eyes full of tears. 'I don't know, you had to go and get yourself . . .' she stopped suddenly, wiped an eye with the back of her hand.

'What did she get herself?' Ciaran asked, his eyes popping, his voice tremulous.

Mam stopped, looked at him. 'Oh, my poor lamb,' she said, taking him in her arms. 'It's awful putting you through this.' She looked at me in disgust, then banged down the lid of the suitcase. Red-faced she said, 'Hurry up, Father Cooney won't wait,' as she carried it out into the hall.

Ciaran followed, wailing, 'I want to go with Stella.'

Mrs Ruane knocked on the door.

'I'm not going to the pictures,' Ciaran said petulantly.

'Of course you are,' she said. 'We're going to have ice cream.'

Father Cooney arrived and rattled his car keys.

'Lovely day for the long drive, Father,' Mrs Ruane said to him.

'Yes, thank God, we're blessed with the weather,' he said, lifting my suitcase and taking it out to his car. I followed him, walking as slowly as possible.

Ciaran ran out ahead of me. 'Don't take Stella away, Father.'

'It's not for ever, lad,' Father Cooney said, taking a shilling out of his pocket and handing it to him.

Ciaran threw it on the ground and howled.

'Shh . . .' Mam said to him, pulling him up as the Brophy children from down the street stopped playing their warrior game and came to stare at us.

Father Cooney continued putting my suitcase in the boot. Ciaran grabbed my arm, and standing on his tippy-toes, his hand cupped over my ear, he said with a sob, 'I'll come and find you.'

Father Cooney practically pushed me into the back of his two-door Morris Minor, such was his hurry to get me away. Mam looked as frightened as a condemned woman going to the gallows as she sat in beside him in the passenger seat. I got into the back seat. As we drove off I looked over my shoulder. Ciaran's small hand was held aloft waving, tears streaming down his face. Mrs Ruane was holding his other hand tightly. I waved to him until we were out of sight.

Ten

The journey to Dublin was long, and the countryside was vast and desolate, nothing but receding fields and dense hedges. Dublin city was full of buildings all jammed together and covered in grime. Even the sky seemed darker. It gave me a tight feeling in my lungs, as if I was deprived of air. Bundled-up people hurried by. I wondered where they were all rushing.

Father Cooney parked inside the entrance gates of an enormous, bleak, four-storey-high barracks of a place. I got out of the car and looked up at its roof, turrets and tall chimneys disappearing into the grey evening mist. I followed Father Cooney and Mam up the echoing concrete steps. A hunchbacked nun, so bent that she barely reached up to my shoulder, answered the door, and shuffled us into the hall. 'Come this way,' she said softly.

We followed her down a long corridor with statues of the Sacred Heart and Our Lady on either side. It smelt of lavender polish and cabbage in the air. She left us in a cold parlour full of shiny brasses.

'Lovely convent,' Mam said, looking around, trying to be cheerful.

'It is indeed,' Father Cooney said congenially.

Another nun came into the room then. We all turned to face her.

'Reverend Mother,' Father Cooney greeted her warmly.

She shook hands briskly with him first, then with Mam as Father Cooney introduced them. Then glancing in my direction, she asked, 'Is this the penitent?'

Father Cooney confirmed with a nod of his head.

'You have brought her to the right place, Father. Here, she will learn how to behave,' Reverend Mother said, giving Father Cooney a look of complicity that seemed to unite them in some conspiracy, leaving Mam looking like an intruder and me feeling that I didn't exist.

'I want to go back home,' I suddenly announced to them all.

Reverend Mother turned to me. 'That's not a good idea,' she said flatly.

I looked pleadingly at Mam but she avoided my eye, standing to one side, retying her headscarf round her neck, an indication to Father Cooney that she wanted to be off.

'I think we'd better go.' Father Cooney led her out of the room.

I followed them down the steps. At the car, while

Father Cooney and Reverend Mother were talking, Mam took a five-pound note out of her purse and wrapped it in her white lace hanky. She slipped it to me. 'Hide that for emergencies, you never know when you might need it. Mind you don't go spending it foolishly, though,' she warned tearfully.

Father Cooney took her arm. 'Compose yourself now, Eileen. Stella will be grand here,' he said to her. He shook me by the hand. 'Goodbye, Stella,' he said gravely, as if he was seeing me for the last time.

I grabbed his arm. 'I don't want to stay here, Father. Please take me home.'

'You know I can't do that.' He shook my hand off and turned away.

Mam shook hands with Reverend Mother and thanked her for taking me in. She gave me a quick kiss on the cheek. 'I'll write and send you the news,' she said, opening the door of the car. She seemed to grow smaller and smaller and more unreachable as she sat into the passenger seat. Father Cooney got in beside her and started the engine.

'Mam! Wait!' I ran after the car as it took off, but her face was hidden behind her scarf and she didn't seem to hear me. She didn't want me any more. I had done a terrible thing.

Once back inside, the hall door tightly shut, I turned to find Reverend Mother and another stern-looking nun waiting for me. Reverend Mother said, 'You know what living the life of a penitent in the Magdalene Laundry means, don't you?'

'No.'

The stern–looking nun stepped forward.

'Is that all you have to say for yourself?' she demanded. 'Aren't you ashamed of what you have done?' She caught me by the scruff of the neck, and wheeled me round to face her. 'You've committed a grave sin. This place is your punishment,' she said, through bared teeth. 'Here you'll do penance and learn the difference between right and wrong. Do you understand?'

'Yes,' I said weakly.

'Yes, Sister!' she corrected. 'Now, get out my sight.'

'Yes, Sister,' I repeated loudly, vowing there and then that whatever happened, whatever was going on inside of me, I wasn't going to show a thing.

The hunchbacked nun appeared then and silently led the way along the corridor, and up a flight of steep stairs, and along another dark corridor with so many rooms leading it off it that I lost count. Then more narrow stairs led to a musty dormitory under the eaves. Two long rows of iron beds were crammed together.

'Make up your bed,' she said kindly, handing me two sheets, and shuffling off.

I covered the lumpy mattress in the rough sheets, then picked up the thin grey blankets from the locker, threw them down on the bed, and pulled them into shape, glad to be doing something that felt homely.

It was quiet. I walked down the centre of the rows of little beds and out into another dark corridor where I found a bathroom with rows of hand basins in the centre, the toilets at the end. I went into one, locked the door, sat down and cried, rocking myself back and forth, thinking of Mam and Father Cooney, miles away by now, leaving me here all alone.

I heard a door open and footsteps coming towards me. I waited. The handle of the toilet door turned. I sat quiet, not making a sound, wary. A girl's voice said, 'I know you're in there.'

I didn't make a sound as I waited for her to go. The handle rattled again. 'You can't stay in there all day. 'I'll give you five minutes, then you better come out.'

Footsteps padded away. Heart hammering, I came out, went to the hand basin, and turned on the tap. It spurted cold water. I splashed my face with it and looked into the dull mirror over the hand basin. I looked a sight.

When I came back into the dormitory there was a tall, pretty girl with fair hair standing by the door. 'Hello. What's your name?' she asked with a brazen smile, pretending not to notice how upset I was.

'Stella.'

'Where are you from?'

'County Wicklow.'

'How old are you?'

'Fifteen.'

'And pregnant,' she said, her eyes on my rounded stomach. 'Boyfriend scraper?'

I looked away.

She went on quizzing me, as if she had to get all the details right. Then she said in a more gentle voice, 'My name is Marie. I'm in charge of the new ones.'

'It's so cramped in here,' I said, looking around.

'Packed like sardines in a tin,' she said.

'I've never been this high up before,' I said, looking out over the rooftops from the window nearest to my bed, where I could see the shops in the village, and stately, red-bricked, terraced houses with long windows, different hall doors, and beautiful gardens.

'You'll get used to it,' she laughed.

I went to open the window to let in some fresh air.

'They're nailed down, you can only open them from the top.'

'Why?'

'In case someone throws themselves out. One girl did many years ago, they say. Sister Luke has the window rod. She's the little nun in charge of this dormitory, the one who brought you up here.'

I shivered. 'What are the other girls like?' I asked.

'Not bad. They're all different types, from all over the country; there are shop girls, office girls, country girls. Mostly they do what they're told and follow the rules because they know what's good for them. A few of the tough ones are hard to deal with. Keep away from them. They could give you a rough time,' she warned.

Marie showed me how to make my bed properly, with hospital corners, and how to fold my clothes neatly. Then she took me up to the attic to stow away my suitcase.

A bell rang.

'Tea time,' said Marie.

'I'm not hungry,' I muttered.

'They'll make you eat whether you want to or not. I'll take you down to the refectory. Come on or we'll be late.'

I heard the sound of doors banging in the distance and a high-pitched voice calling out as I followed her down a different flight of stairs. 'I'll never find my way back up there,' I said to her.

'Shh.' She put her finger to her lips as we passed the chapel.

Outside a big, heavy door clumps of girls stood in drab, navy-blue overalls, talking in hushed tones. We joined them. A nun appeared from nowhere and ordered, 'Silence'. A few girls started pushing and shoving when the door opened. With a face like a thunder, the nun clapped her hands and waved us into line, like a policeman controlling traffic. A long queue formed.

In the refectory, a girl in a white coat was ladling out watery stew from an enormous urn. There were stacks of enamel bowls beside her. I took one and held it out. I was given a thick slice of hard bread to go with it. The long wooden table filled up. Marie and I sat together, opposite three girls who were whispering, heads close together. They kept their eyes averted to let me know that I wasn't part of their group. From the corners of my eyes I watched them as I struggled to eat the greasy mess that tasted of boiled rags – but it warmed me up. A girl at the end of the table was crying. Marie whispered, 'That's Sadie. She has to give her baby up tomorrow,' she added.

After supper we said prayers in the chapel. At nine o'clock sharp we went up to the dormitory. Sister Luke called the roll and said the night prayers. I pulled the flimsy curtain round my bed, got undressed, into my pyjamas, and folded my clothes neatly at the bottom of the bed. I struggled down between the ice-cold sheets and pulled the grey blankets up under my chin. I was so close to the girl in the next bed that I could have reached out and touched her if I'd wanted to.

Through the flimsy curtain I looked out at the moon, round and yellow against the black sky, and the stars around it – unshed tears stuck in my throat. I thought of Mam at home, getting Ciaran ready for bed. I breathed in to stop myself from crying, picturing Mam in her coloured, Sunday frock, standing by the window; the curve of the moon was her hair. She was so real to me that I wanted to reach out to take her hand and bring her down into the bed. I must have fallen asleep eventually and woke to the sound of someone crying at the end of the dormitory. I wondered if it was Sadie. I looked at the window for Mam, certain that she was still there, but the pale morning light had dissolved her, leaving me alone in a chilly, no man's land. I cried myself back to sleep before we were all brutally awoken by a nun bursting into the dormitory, calling out, 'Benedict Camas Domino'.

I struggled to open my eyes, squinting up at her, lost for a moment, not knowing where I was. She leaned over me.

'You, get up!' she ordered.

My stomach churning, I put on my dressing gown and picked my way through the half-darkness, terrified that I'd bump into something. Girls in raggy dressing gowns stumbled past, sleepy-eyed and white-faced. One girl with matted hair almost collided with me. 'You're new,' she said, cocking her head and looking at me with half-shut eyes.

'Yes.'

'Hurry up or you'll be in trouble,' she whispered, indicating the hand basins.

The water was freezing. I dressed hurriedly and followed the others to the chapel. After mass we queued up silently for breakfast. The nun from the previous evening supervised the doling out of some grey liquid which bore little resemblance to porridge, but that, apparently, was what it was. The tea from an urn was bitter, the bread again hard.

After breakfast and bed-making and tidying of the dormitory, Sister Luke took the roll call, sent two girls off to the kitchen to peel potatoes and vegetables, and two to polish the brasses in the parlour, pointing them out at random, saying, 'You and you.'

The rest of us were divided between the Laundry and the Wash House. Because I was a new girl I was sent to the Wash House.

Eleven

The Wash House was an enormous, high-ceilinged room, drenched with steam. There was the strong tang of carbolic soap everywhere. Along one side of it were four tall, many-paned, barred windows, above a row of sinks mounted on a wall the colour of earth. Copper pipes, clotted with dirt and grime, gasped and gurgled. Over the door hung a large painting of the Crucifixion; the dying eyes of Jesus stared out at me. The sad face of Mary, his mother, standing at the foot of the cross, made me think of Mam.

Girls moved around speedily as if they were running for cover from the fierce nun who stood blocking the door, her back poker-stiff. She wore a long white apron over her turned-up habit, the sleeves of which were encased in white covers that looked like long bread loaves. Her pinned-back veil made her nose sharp like a question mark. Her steely blue eyes were watchful.

'I'm Sister Michael,' she said.

'Hello Sister,' I said.

'You do not address me unless I give you permission

to do so,' she said sternly, and handed me a navy-blue housecoat. I struggled into it and felt her corpse-cold hands touch mine as she straightened it all the way down, almost to my ankles.

'Stella Wood is no more. From now on your name is Star, after Our Lady, Star of the Sea. Now, follow me,' she commanded, her rustling habit brushing past me as she made her way to the row of sinks.

'This is yours,' she said. 'Dolores will show you what to do.'

A lanky, frail-looking girl handed me a basket of dirty sheets. She turned on the taps, fiddling with them to get the right temperature, then slipped a sheet in hot water and began washing them.

'Begin with the stains,' she said, rubbing a bar of Sunlight carbolic soap across one. Her hands were as red as lobsters. 'Now, you do it.'

The sheets bobbed to the surface as I struggled with them. Dolores watched over me as I scrubbed them until my own hands were red and aching.

As we worked Sister Michael walked up and down saying prayers, her eyes on me. 'Oh, Lord, remove from me all darkness of sin and ignorance. Instruct my tongue and pour into my lips the grace of thy blessing,' she prayed.

'Now rinse them out,' Dolores told me.

With aching hands I rinsed them, pulled down so heavily by their weight that I had to clutch the edge of the sink. I dragged a bucket to the mangle and rolled each sheet through it evenly, watching the water spurt out in tiny jets of water as they fed through. Desperately I thought of Charles, and wondered where he was at that minute, and what he was doing, and if he ever thought about me. Sister Michael came and stood behind me. 'You've dropped this,' she said, holding out a wet pillowcase.

'Thank you, Sister.' My throat tightened as I inhaled the steamy air to stop myself from crying.

Sister Michael swung away with a loping stride and Dolores took the sheets to the clothesline. When she returned she stayed at her own sink, zipped into her own world, a frown on her face. The girl on the other side of me talked to herself as she worked. Occasionally she laughed out loud. Further along, through the damp, soggy atmosphere, a child-like woman was starching collars, swishing the starch rhythmically to and fro, staring blankly in front of her. I pressed the wet pillowcase to my face. Behind it, I continued to cry.

All day, I kept my hands moving in the acrid water, thrashing the washing around until it turned grey and stinking. I lifted the garments up and dropped them back down again, rubbed in carbolic soap and scrubbed them. The air was gassy with the smell of washing and the stench of the water in the sink was sickening. I piled up another batch of mangled sheets in a bucket and carried it outside to the clothesline.

I pegged up the washing, patting down the slimy material. The sun touched the sheets and the wind whipped them up. I stood back and watched them flapping about in pointless circles, the wind transforming them into shape of tigers' tails. Suspended in the air, the trailing sheets spoke to me in a sign language as they waved in the thin breeze. As the sun touched them, they weren't sheets any more but the shadows of Mam, Dad and Ciaran. I looked at the Daddy sheet, blowing towards me then receding as though he were ashamed of me. I wasn't his 'Rising Star' any more. I was his 'Fallen Star'. The Mammy sheet was creased and sad-looking. The child sheet at the end of the line waved frantically at me as it blew in the wind. 'Hello Stella, goodbye Stella,' it was saying.

A girl who barely reached up to my shoulder helped me take my next bucket-load of washing to the clothesline. 'I'm Janet,' she said, standing on an upturned crate to hang up the washing.

'I'm Stella – I mean Star.'

She grinned and I saw her teeth were yellow. 'When's your baby due?'

'January.'

'That's a long way off. Mine's due next month.' She teetered on the crate and nearly fell off.

'Here,' I smiled. I'll hang these up; you take in the dry ones. I handed them down to her.

The garden was welcoming after the overheated Wash

House. I hung the sheets up slowly, listening as the voices of children playing in the schoolyard nearby floated over the high walls. I thought of Ciaran playing tag with the other boys in his schoolyard and missing me. Suddenly, weak-kneed with sadness I sat on a low wall and watched the crisp sheets shift and billow in the breeze like the pale lustrous curtains in Charles's bedroom that had sheltered us from the world as we made love. I wiped my eyes and looked around.

Behind the convent there was a narrow lane. Through the barred gates two boys scuffled past, calling to one another. One boy threw pebbles up to one of the windows, maybe hoping to attract the attention of the girls. An old man sitting on a bench shouted after them to stop their carry-on.

The sun struck the windows of the distant church beyond. It beckoned to me with its bright glow. I wanted to get out of this jungle of wet clothes and sad girls, into the streets where there were no bars and locks, where cars were changing gears at traffic lights and life was normal.

The sound of a clanging bell brought me back to reality. There was no escape. Nowhere to go but back to the Wash House and another pile of filthy sheets.

'What took you so long?' Sister Michael snapped. 'What were you doing out there?'

'I was hanging up the washing.'

'And what else?'

'Nothing.'

'Were you smoking?'

'No.'

'I don't believe you.' She gave me a clout with her beads. They stung my head. 'Get on with it, no time to waste.'

Next morning I returned to the Wash House and delved into a new pile of dirty laundry, to begin the vigorous scrubbing and the mangling all over again. Dolores handed me a mop and a bucket of water and asked me to help her to wash the floor.

I swished the mop across the slippery floor, my hands clammy on the handle, my overall stuck to my legs in the heat. Even the air tasted hot in the back of my throat.

Dolores tried to open one of the windows to let in some air. Sister Michael glided up to her. 'What do you think you are doing?' she demanded.

Dolores said, 'This winda's stuck.'

'Leave it, get on with your work,' Sister Michael commanded.

'But it's boilin' in here, Sister,' Dolores complained.

'Put up with it. You're lucky to have a roof over your head, food, and a bed to sleep in. There's many a one in your situation roughing it on the streets,' Sister Michael said.

Dolores daringly stuck out her tongue at the nun behind her back. Sister Michael turned and caught her. She whacked her knuckles with the heavy rosary beads that hung from her waist and marched off, leaving Dolores snivelling.

With so many flights of stairs, and corridors branching off in all directions I kept getting lost. I couldn't ask directions because talking was forbidden, except in dire emergency. The girls managed to communicate in some shape or form. They used their own version of sign language and mouthed to one another. Pressing two fingers to your lips and pulling them away a couple of times meant, 'Let's go out for a sneaky smoke'. Kissing your bunched-up fingers behind Sister Michael's back meant, 'Feck her.' Rocking an imaginary baby in your arms meant, 'Have you heard any news of your baby?'

Each day the 'press work' was sent to the Ironing Room in a big wash house trolley. We took it in turns to push the trolley over to the Ironing Room. The day I took the trolley over, the 'hand-ironer' in charge took it from me. She was a big, plump, red-faced girl with long, straggly hair, and was propped behind an ironing board.

'I haven't seen *you* before,' she said, sizing me up. 'What's your name?'

'Stella.'

'I'm Bernadette. Why are *you* here?'

'The same reason as everyone else,' I said.

'You're a cheeky young one,' she said, eyeing me up and down before dismissing me.

★ ★ ★

The following day I was at the sink when Bernie's head emerged from behind a pile of laundry. 'I've you to thank for this shabby lot,' she said, her neck twisting like a turtle's from its carapace to indicate the pile of grey-looking washing on the floor. 'See what I'm talkin' about?' She leaned towards me, her hands on her hips. 'Are you trying to ruin the good reputation of this laundry or wha'?' There was a threatening look in her protruding eyes.

I stood in silence, terrified.

'Did you hear me?'

'Yes.'

'You'd better come and explain yourself to Sister Michael, and bring that filth with you.'

I picked up the bundle of clothes she'd dropped and, sheep-like, I followed her down the aisle. Girls looked up curiously as she swayed past them.

Sister Michael was in her office. Bernie marched me in and showed her the grey washing, indicating me. 'This is her work. How am I expected to send it out, Sister?' she said.

Sister Michael nodded her head. 'Disgraceful. Thank you Bernadette, I'll deal with it.'

With a smug grin at me, Bernie left.

'Well, what have you to say for yourself?' Sister Michael asked, her eyes boring into me.

'I . . .' my tongue faltered, my throat closed over. No answer came out.

She came forward. 'You're going to be trouble, I can tell,' she snorted, and whacked me across the face.

I reeled backwards. The heat of the room blazed up into my head; I thought I was going to faint.

'Look at the cut of you, you're a disgrace,' she said, her measuring eyes taking me in.

I was suddenly conscious of my untidy appearance. The itchy Lyle stockings, the streaky, damp overall.

'That's all you're getting, just this once,' she said. 'Now go and do that washing again, *properly* this time.' Her knuckley hand smoothed down my overall.

'Thank you, Sister.' I felt unsteady as I walked away, my cheeks burning.

When the bell clanged we lined up at the door, our work done for the day. I tried to eat the fatty meat and lumpy potatoes, hungry for Mam's succulent chips and a slice of her rhubarb tart. I wanted to be sitting by the fire at home. I wondered if Mam was missing me? I knew Ciaran would be.

That evening, in the chapel, I went over my day: the Wash House, the dirty washing, the sad girls in their navy-blue housecoats. I looked at the nuns in the choir with their angelic faces, absorbed in their prayers. They chanted:

> *My soul glorifies the Lord,*
> *My spirit rejoices in God, my Saviour.*
> *He looks on his servant in her lowliness;*
> *Henceforth all ages will call me blessed.'*

Could these be the same nuns who paraded the Wash House with their huge beads and long leather straps dangling from their waists and who gave me a strange, prickly feeling on my skin. In prayer they looked different. These were holy women. No one ever questioned their word. It was law.

I looked around at all the tired-faced girls, eyes staring and blank, their lips moving in prayer, and realised that we were all prisoners, doomed for ever to bow to the will of the Sisters. For the first time I understood what it meant to be a pillar of the church.

Would I ever get used to them? Would I ever manage to keep out of trouble? I doubted it.

The following Saturday, Sister Luke inspected the dormitory. She checked for forbidden sweets and cigarettes in the lockers, under the mattresses, and behind the curtains, Marie said, 'They're checking for knives and razors, too.'

On Sunday morning I put on my best blue dress that Mam had made for my birthday. The sleeves bunched up under my arms, the waist was tight. Sister Michael, standing in the corridor, considered me as if I was from another planet.

The 'shop' was opened for a half an hour in the afternoon. The nun in charge sold soap, toothpaste and cigarettes in limited supply to the older women. The girls who had money sent from relatives would pull each

others' coats off in their frenzy to get a packet. I didn't go
in. I was saving my fiver for when my baby was born.

Dear Mam,
I am fine. I made friends with one of the girls. Her child has
been taken away from her. Everybody here is very unhappy,
including me.

I sucked the tip of my biro, not knowing what else to say.
The girl next to me tapped her foot. I looked up. She
made faces and pointed at the nun at the desk, then at my
letter, screwing up her face, shaking her head. I tore it up
and wrote:

Dear Mam,
I am settling down, but I miss you so much, I think about you
all the time. Please come and see me as soon as you are up to it.

Dear Ciaran,
I'm sure you are all excited about your birthday. I'll send you a
present later on when I get a chance to go to the shops. How are
you enjoying your school holidays? I wish I were there to take
you to the beach. I think of you all of the time. Promise you
won't forget me.

As I wrote, I pictured Ciaran and Mam sitting at the
kitchen table eating their dinner together, the smell of
cooking all through the house. I could hear the sound of

Ciaran's ball bouncing off the back wall and his little legs running after it. The tears dropped down on to the page in great big splodges and I had to start all over again.

Twelve

After a few weeks of working as hard as I could in the Wash House I was promoted to the Laundry. Another high-ceilinged, old building. The entrance was full of large hampers from long-standing customers. Each morning they were lifted to the side of the sorter's stall. There she would check off the list in each book.

'This information is for office use so that articles can be priced,' Patricia, the girl in charge, explained to me. 'Also, it is an important guide to the packer when she checks out the laundry.'

Linen was divided into different categories: sheets, tablecloths, coloured and white shirts, towels, and shop coats were weighed dry to allocate cost and separated. Blankets were washed in large, old machines. A girl on the tabbing machine marked articles torn or badly stained with red cotton at the point of damage. Red thread was used to indicate starching required. A red-and-blue thread was used to identify items for light starching. Fine material, such as delicate silk, was marked by a piece of white cotton tape with the customer's registered mark in black indelible ink.

Sister Perpetua was the nun in charge; she stalked the aisles every ten minutes, her black shoes squeaking as she walked, her terrifying eyes as hard as polished stones behind her steel-rimmed spectacles. She ruled by fear, shrieking out instructions, and making her point with sharp strokes of her outstretched hand, her coif billowing, sometimes poking the slackers in the back with a set of keys that hung from a leather strap at her waist.

The bulk of the linen was sent up to the Ironing Room by a hand-operated service lift. There was a covered passage joining the Ironing Room to the Packing Room, where the clean laundry was sorted and tied up into brown-paper packages, then sent out to the back lobby for the van driver to collect. I was allocated to the Ironing Room where help was urgently needed.

'You're the cheeky one,' Bernie said when she saw me coming. 'We'll have to put manners on her, won't we, girls?' She looked around at the others.

'That'll be no bother,' one of them said out of the side of her mouth.

Bernie smirked. I backed away.

'Don't be scared. As long as you make yourself useful and do a good job, you'll be all right,' she said.

'And don't think you'll get out of here either,' the smirking girls said.

'Yeah, you'll be here for good,' Bernie agreed, a sloping

grin loitering on her shiny face.

That thought hadn't even occurred to me. Now it struck me with a jolt as I watched her at work. Beads of perspiration dotted her brow as she rolled her iron back and forth over a lace garment. Her job was the 'finery'. She was a craftswoman and knew her worth.

She put down her iron and took me to an ironing board facing the window. Handing me a basket of clothes, she took a shirt from the top of the pile and put it under my nose. 'Start with this. You better be good,' she warned.

I glanced round at the hot shiny faces of the other girls with the same feeling of panic I'd had on my first day in the Wash House. They worked on, their eyes downcast. Every nerve in my body jangled as I tried to copy what they were doing.

After a short while Bernie came and stood over me. 'You think that's proper ironing, do you?' she enquired as I pressed the iron down hard on the collar.

'I don't know how to iron,' I said, not knowing what else to say.

She spun round to face me. 'Are you serious?'

'I've never had to do it,' I said, helplessly.

'Oh, so you've been gently reared, have you? You're a cut above everyone else are you, Miss Snooty Drawers?' she goaded, a smirk on her face. She moved closer. 'Well, let me tell you something. This Ironing Room has high standards and you'd never meet them.'

'Sister Michael thinks I'm a good worker,' I said.

'Oh, are you her little pet?' she teased, looking at me closely. 'Wait until I tell her that you're no good,' she hissed into my ear.

'Then teach me how to iron properly or send me back,' I retorted before I could stop myself.

Someone giggled.

'Less of your cheek,' she said, giving me a clout across the face.

One of the girls walked over to us. 'I'll show her how,' she offered.

Bernie handed her my iron. 'You watch and learn from Greta,' she warned and marched off.

Greta said, 'You'll pick it up in no time. I hadn't a clue when I started here either. It takes practice and patience.' With a slow smooth glide up then down, she ironed the front of the shirt and the collar. Handing the iron to me, she said, 'Now you have a go. Take your time. You'll soon got the hang of it.'

'Thanks,' I said, grateful for her gentleness.

I started on the back of the shirt, running the iron up and down jerkily, my insides churning. With a shake of her head Greta put her hand over mine and guided the iron smoothly, warning me again not to hurry. As I ran it along, her experienced eyes followed my every move. As the smell of hot cotton rose up into the air it blew up memories of childhood – of Mam at her ironing board, a mountain of washing fresh from the clothesline beside her, waiting for her expert touch.

Next, I tackled a white poplin blouse similar to Mam's Sunday-going-to-mass one. So I gently patted down the creases on the front, trickled the iron between the covered buttons, lingering on the pocket and the cuffs. Finally, I caressed the scalloped collar, carefully stroking out the puckers with the tip of my iron. Greta nodded her approval, and handed me another shirt. Pleased with the result she left me to continue on my own, advising me not to hurry the job. 'Less haste, more speed,' she said with a smile.

When I finally put down my iron, it was with confidence that I delivered my basket of smooth, clean laundry to Bernie for inspection. I could feel the eyes of the other girls on me as she examined it.

'That's an improvement,' she said grudgingly, handing me another bundle to do.

'Thank you for helping me,' I whispered to Greta as I passed her, my heart light with relief. She gave my arm a squeeze.

From then on I ironed all day, every day. But the monotony did nothing to wipe out memories of home. Each day, as I worked, I retreated into those memories and fed on them like a vampire sucking blood. Mam's voice was in the crackle of the iron, her smile was in the crest of a seam. Each day I ironed Dad's shoulders into the shirts, straightening out his back and arms along the sleeves. I pressed Mam in the pleats of skirts and hung on to them like I did when I was a small child. I ironed the creases out of her neck and the furrows from her brow in the collars of blouses. The hiss of the iron was a kiss on Ciaran's cheek.

Each day Bernie slunk about, checking everything. She would nod her approval as she examined every detail of my work. 'You're coming on well,' she said one day, her eyes lacking their usual contempt. I never spoke for fear of another clout, but her praise was encouraging. All day, every day I ironed, trapping my grief in every seam. The air baked with the smell of hot clothes. Often, during the day I would feel faint in the heat, and would stop to take a deep breath. There were no complaints from Bernie about this, or about the quality of my work. Being assigned to the Ironing Room was turning out to be the best thing that had happened to me since my arrival in the Magdalene Laundry.

Or so I thought, until one morning when Bernie floated up to me with a jumble of clothes under her arm and said, 'This batch belongs to a very important customer. I want you to do it because you're by far the best.'

Thrilled with the compliment, I set to work. Slowly, I ironed the stiff, starched collars and the grandfather shirts. I took the greatest care over the fancy lace tablecloths and matching napkins. I ran my iron smoothly up and down a long, white lawn frock, more beautiful than anything I had ever seen. Gently I patted the elasticised smocking across the front. The swaying trees outside the window caught my eyes. I imagined the owner of this dress to be a young girl. I pictured her wreathed in smiles as she trailed into a ballroom and swayed around the floor with a handsome young man, the folds of her frock billowing. I thought of Maeve and the parties we'd gone to in our lovely frocks. Thinking of the secrets we'd shared, I hoped that all of it wouldn't be forgotten by the time I saw her again. I was wondering how she was getting on and what she was doing for the summer, when the smell of burning snapped me out of my reverie. I looked down to see, to my horror, a long, brown scorch mark on the fine smocking.

'I smell burning.'

Before I had time to hide it Bernie was coming towards me, her nostrils flaring, like a sniffer dog.

Too late, I folded over the damaged smocking.

'You stupid lump,' she cried, lifting the dress to the light. 'Look what you've done. I saw you daydreaming out the winda' instead of concentrating on your work.'

She slapped me hard across the face. I twisted my head away from her but fell backwards and slid down the wall. I lay sprawled on the ground, dazed and shivering.

'Get up, you useless slut,' she shouted, grabbing my hair, pulling me to my feet by its roots. I tried to push her away but it was like trying to shift a brick wall. She hit me again, harder this time. A groan escaped me. I clutched my stomach. 'I knew you were trouble the minute I laid eyes on you, with your cheeky tongue and your airs and graces. One more mistake and I'll give you more than a slap. Understand?' Another smack across the face knocked the breath out of me. The room spun.

'Hey, what's going on here?' came a muffled voice. When I focused I saw Marie standing over me.

'I'd keep out of this if I were you,' Bernie scowled at her.

Marie said to Bernie, 'What did she do?'

'She only scorched a frock that came from Aras An Uachtaran – President De Valera's family's ironing no less. Gazing out the winda when she should have been watching what she was doing.' Bernie showed Marie the scorch mark.

Marie took the dress from her saying she'd 'fix it'. Turning to me she asked, 'Are you OK?'

Feeling faint, I shook my head.

'Don't mind her, she's putting on an act for your benefit,' Bernie said.

Calmly, Marie led me towards the door.

'Where are you taking her?' Bernie's voice was high-pitched with rage as she blocked the door.

'To the Infirmary, and if you ever as much as lay a finger on her again you'll be sorry,' Marie warned her.

'Who'll make me?' Bernie said daringly.

'I will, you big fat bully. Now get out of my way,'

Marie said, pushing her aside.

'Are you threatening me?' A malicious smile played on Bernie's lips as she leaped forward again.

'If you'd rather I reported you to Reverend Mother, that's fine with me,' Marie said calmly.

'Oh! I'm quaking in my shoes!' Bernie laughed. 'That one's nothing but trouble,' she added, glancing in my direction.

'I'll deal with her,' Marie said with authority, leading me out of the room, her arm around me.

'And you needn't bother sending her back here,' Bernie shouted after her.

Once out of the room I said, 'I'm sorry, Marie. I didn't do it on purpose.'

'I know that,' she said, her arm supporting me as we walked down the corridor.

'I can't stand it,' I began to cry. 'I'm scared to death of her. She's been picking on me from the start and I don't understand why.'

'Don't mind that big fat lump of lard. She's too much of a coward to pick on the older girls. You're an easy target.'

'It's not just her, it's everything,' I sobbed.

'Don't let that big blabbermouth get the better of you. Let's go and find Sister Angela. She can have a look at that gash on the side of your head.'

Sister Angela bathed and bandaged my head. For the rest of the day I was allowed to go to bed and rest. 'Say a

127

prayer for the girl who hit you,' Sister Angela said soothingly, tucking me into my little bed with a hot cup of sweet tea.

I didn't pray for Bernie, but I thought about prayer and God and how the nuns in school had drummed into us that God was everywhere. 'He is in our hearts and minds, we are all his people, he makes no difference between us,' they had said. I wondered why God made such differences between us girls and the nuns. Surely he was supposed to love us all equally and treat us all the same?

I listened to the clock ticking, the pipes murmuring, and thought about my baby. Examining my bruises, I worried that Bernie might have damaged it. Would I survive here and the nuns until the baby's birth? I said this to Marie when she came to see me.

'Feeling sorry for yourself won't get you anywhere,' she said. 'The trick is not to react to any of them. Say, 'Yes Sister . . . no Sister . . . three bags full Sister . . .' to all of them, all of the time, like I do. Don't forget we're all in the same boat.

Thirteen

After my disaster in the Ironing Room I was transferred to the Packing Room. My new job was to check each item of laundry off lists of names and addresses, and separate the bundles for packaging.

The first time that I was sent to the back lobby with the brown-paper parcels, the delivery boy was standing by his van, waiting patiently. He was tall and lanky, and his hands stuck out of his too-short-sleeved brown coat.

'Hello, I'm Danny,' he said.

'I'm Stella, sorry for the delay.' I handed over the trolley full of parcels.

'Don't worry about it,' he said, and smiled. 'I haven't seen you before, have I?' he added.

'No, I've not been here long. I've been working in the Ironing Room.'

'Settling in OK?' he asked.

'Not really.'

'Yeah, I know what you mean.' He glanced past me, making it clear from his disapproving expression that he knew what the Magdalene Laundry was like and what the girls were going through. 'So where are you from?' he asked as he signed the delivery book.

'County Wicklow.'

'What in God's name possessed your parents to send you up here?'

'Mam asked our parish priest for advice when . . .' I looked down at my stomach, my face on fire. 'He brought me here.'

Danny raised his eyes to heaven. 'Bad decision,' he said, shaking his head. 'You're too young to be in this place.'

'If my dad had been there he wouldn't have agreed to it. He doesn't like Father Cooney.'

'Where is your dad?'

'Working in England. He doesn't know I'm here.'

'Hurry up,' Patricia, the girl in charge of the lobby, called out.

Danny shut the van door with a bang and handed me back the book.

'If you want to write to your da or anyone I'll post the letter for you,' he said in a low voice.

'Thank you,' I said in surprise.

'I post letters for most of the girls. Some get them sent to my address. They're desperate for news from home. Any time you want a letter posted, give it to me – but be very careful, there are one or two sneaks around who'll tell the nuns if they see you,' he said under his breath.

That night, in bed, I wrote to Charles by the light of the moon.

Dear Charles,
Please come and get me out of here. All I need is for you to claim me, then I can leave. I'll find a job and won't make any demands on you, I promise, and I'll keep our baby away from you so you won't have to have anything to do with us.
   Stella

Marie supplied the stamp and the next evening I gave it to Danny to post. He pretended to read the notice board as he took the letter and put it in his pocket, then he took the deliveries, packed them into his van, signed the book in his spidery hand, and drove off saying, 'I'll see you tomorrow'.

Next I wrote to Mam, asking her to write back to me at Danny's address with all the news, and begging her to come and see me. She wrote to the convent address saying that she'd try to get up to see me on the Sunday. I waited all day long, going up to the dormitory, looking out the window, my eyes on the gate, waiting for her. When I saw Father Cooney's car arriving I ran downstairs without waiting to be sent for.

'Where's Mam?' I asked, looking at the empty passenger seat.

'She couldn't come,' he said. 'She has a touch of flu and she didn't want to pass it on to you. She said to tell you she's asking for you.' He handed me a bag of toffees and a pound note. 'She sent you these.'

I hated crying in front of him, but I couldn't stop

myself. 'I want to go home,' I miss Mam and Ciaran,' I wailed, my voice catching in my breath.

Father Cooney looked away, embarrassed. 'I'm disappointed in you, Stella, acting the baby like this, and the nuns so good to you.'

'The nuns are horrible; I hate it here,' I blurted out.

Shocked, he turned to me. 'How can you say such a terrible thing? It must be your state of mind at the moment. You'll be grand when . . . in a little while, when it's all over.'

'I won't be grand, Father, I know I won't. I want to go home now.'

He wasn't listening. He was walking ahead of me up the steps and into the parlour, his head in the air. Miserable, I followed him and was allowed to sit with him while he thanked the nuns for their charity and kindness. As soon as Sister Luke brought in the tea tray I was dismissed.

Next evening, I was talking to Danny when the outside door opened and Sister Perpetua appeared.

'What are you doing out here in the dark?' she asked.

'We were checking off the list, Sister. There's an extra load today,' Danny said, putting his biro back behind his ear and stuffing parcels busily into the back of his van.

'Well, hurry up and get back to the work,' she ordered me.

Later she said to me. 'You are forbidden to hold a

132

conversation with the delivery boy. If I catch you talking to him again I'll send you back to the Wash House.'

From then on I had to communicate with Danny in whispers or sign language. I caught a cold from going from the hot Packing Room to the freezing-cold lobby. My throat was so sore that I couldn't swallow. At dinner the following Sunday, I took a mouthful of cabbage and gagged at the rotten, watery taste of it. 'It's pig slop,' I said to the girl next to me.

The nun in charge heard my remark. 'For that, you can eat it,' she ordered. She stood over me until I took a mouthful. A lump of grizzly meat caught in my throat and stuck there. I couldn't stop myself. I vomited all over the floor. Her patience lost, the nun sent me up to the Infirmary.

Sister Angela examined me and took my temperature. She said that it was high and that she thought I was coming down with a fever. Scared that I might infect the rest of the girls in my dormitory, she put me in a tiny room on the corridor where the nuns slept – called a cell.

From the window of my cell I could see the girls coming and going, walking despondently in a straggly crocodile: short girls, tall girls, some with the hems of their frocks dipping, all looking miserable. Sister Perpetua would march along behind them, her steel-rimmed spectacles glinting in the sunshine. I could hear their despondent voices as they recited the

Sorrowful Mysteries of the Rosary, and was glad I was missing it.

I fell asleep and didn't wake up until evening time. I hopped out of bed and went to my window to look out to see what was going on outside.

Children were playing ball in a garden a short distance away. A man and woman were walking along the road, arm in arm. Above me was the parapet. I imagined myself climbing out of the window and pulling myself up on to the roof. There, I'd be free of the convent. I'd flap my arms like a bird and fly up into the air, perch on one of the convent chimneys and peer down from the roof of the ugly building and frighten the nuns to death. Then I'd take off over the rooftops, the church spire, fly past houses and shops, skim the tops of trees on my way to the green fields and blue hills of home. I rattled the window. It was jammed shut.

'Don't!' The tea tray in Sister Angela's hands wobbled with fright when she saw me trying to open the window. 'If you try to take your own life it is a grave sin, graver than the one you've already committed.'

'I wasn't going to do away with myself, Sister,' I said.

She didn't believe me. 'Get back into bed before you catch pneumonia, and have some tea.'

She placed the tray on the locker beside my bed. I thanked her, and sipped the tea gratefully. I left the bread. It was too hard to swallow.

That night I dreamed that I was trapped in a dark place

and tied up with ropes. I woke up with a scream in my throat. Frightened, I sat up in bed, waiting for someone to come and punish me for screaming, but no one came near me.

The next morning Sister Angela brought me a bowl of porridge, but my throat felt as if a sharp knife was stuck in it when I tried to eat.

The doctor was sent for. He diagnosed tonsillitis, and prescribed poultices on the neck and chest, and cold compresses on the forehead to reduce the temperature. Sister Angela was very kind to me. She nursed me with the gentleness of a mother. Each day she brought me cold drinks and put painful poultices on my neck. For a week I lay there, alternately shivering and sweating.

One night I dreamed about Mam. As I awoke I heard the sound of her shoes in the creak of the door, saw her gaze in the first rays of the morning sunshine that streamed through the grimy window. Joyously, I called out, 'Mam!' But it was only Sister Angela with my breakfast.

'You're delirious,' she said, with a worried frown.

The fever dropped. Slowly I got better and I got used to my cell. It was nicer than the overcrowded dormitory, and I had the magpies and pigeons on the roof and the spiders in their webs in the eaves for my companions. I would watch a helpless fly being slowly folded into a web by the long deft legs of a spider, and I would feel a great sympathy for the plight of the poor fly, knowing that no matter how hard it struggled there was no escape.

Often at night a shout from the street, or a car changing gear, or a barking dog would trigger a memory of home and make me cry. In this tiny space I learned to practise patience and silence.

As soon as I felt better I was sent back to work. Weak and run-down, I found it hard to keep up with my jobs. I got sores on my head: big, itchy red spots that turned septic from scratching them. One morning after breakfast, Marie said to me, 'Go and get your coat. We're going to the chemist to get you something to clear up those sores. An hour out of here won't do you any hard now, will it?' She smiled, aiming a meaningful glance at me. 'You haven't seen Donnybrook yet.'

'How can I go out in public looking like this?' I asked plaintively.

'I'll get you a scarf to cover your head.'

At the entrance we passed the nun on guard duty. Marie told her where we were going. It had been so long since I'd been out that my legs shook as we walked out into the street. I slunk by the railings, my heart thumping. It began to rain. Marie took an umbrella out of her shopping bag and held it above our heads like a shield. 'This is fun. I love the rain, don't you?' she said, half-skipping along, her curls bouncing as she went.

Donnybrook village was busy with traffic. Horns

honked, people slid past, their faces hidden under their umbrellas. Marie stopped at the newsagent's to buy cigarettes and matches, and remarked to the lady on the till about the awful weather as she lit up. As soon as we were back on the street she hissed, 'Look out, there's Father Cronin, the parish priest, at the bus stop. We don't want him to see us, he'll tell the nuns that I was smoking.' She dragged me down a side street. We hid in the doorway of a betting office. The rain made a plopping noise as it ran off the gutter beside me. A bus backfired as it came to a halt, splashing the pavement. Father Cronin got on it and it drove off.

We continued on our way, stopping to admire beautiful dresses in one shop window and shoes in another. Finally, we arrived at a red-bricked house with 'Surgery' written over the door. As we waited in the queue for the doctor I shrank into a corner, scared that I had leprosy or some other humiliating disease.

Marie laughed and said, 'Don't be such a cowardy-custard.'

My turn finally came. The nice doctor examined my head, told Marie that I had Impetigo, and prescribed ointment for it. 'You must eat plenty of greens and drink milk to build you up,' he said to me.

'That's a laugh,' Marie said to me on our way out. 'Imagine ordering that lot from the nuns. Come on, there's a nice café round the corner. They serve delicious hot chocolate.'

My stomach growled. 'Just what I need,' I said. 'But I haven't got any money.'

'I have,' she said. I haven't run errands for the nuns all these years for nothing. I've learned a few tricks of the trade.' She took out her purse and rattled it. We continued along the busy thoroughfare and scampered gratefully into the shelter of the café. In the mirror on the door I caught sight of my reflection and was shocked at my appearance. I hadn't realised how much I showed. Marie walked confidently between white-clothed tables, selecting one in a corner. The all-pervasive smell of coffee reminded of Irene's café and I felt a lump in my throat as I followed her.

A big, smiley woman with a heavily powdered face wobbled over to us. 'Hello Marie, good to see you again,' she said.

'Howya Kitty, could we have two hot chocolates and two cream buns, please?' Marie's face glistened from the rain; her hair hung in wet waves. She looked very pretty as she gave the orders.

'You can of course, love. Coming up in a jiffy,' Kitty said, and went off.

She delivered the delicious-smelling hot chocolate and buns to us quickly.

'Thanks.' Marie coughed.

'You'd want to watch that cough. It's a graveyard one,' Kitty said, with concern. 'Have you taken anything for it?'

Marie shook her head. 'It's only a tickle in my throat,' she smiled, but she'd turned a deathly pale, except for two red blotches on her cheeks.

Kitty said, 'Go into the lavvy and dry your hair with the towel there.'

Marie threw her eyes up to the ceiling. 'Don't fuss, Kitty, I'm grand,' she said.

'Take your coats off, make yourselves comfortable.'

'We don't want to frighten the public with the sight of our awful overalls, Marie said, sipping her coffee and biting into one of the cream buns.

'And how are the good nuns?' Kitty said sarcastically.

Marie half-covered her mouth as she said, 'If they knew we were here scoffing cream cakes they'd have us tortured. Look at this nice, poor harmless young girl here,' she said, nodding at me. 'She's only a child and they have her worked to the bone. You know what'll happen to her?'

'She'll go mad like the rest of those poor girls.' Kitty said.

I was too busy stuffing my mouth to care.

'What a place to find yourself in,' Kitty tut-tutted in sympathy, her eyes on me. 'No wages for the terrible long hours you put in.'

'Not even a decent square meal,' Marie complained. 'Stella here has been very sick.'

'There's no rhyme or reason to it,' Kitty agreed.

Marie smiled: 'I'm all for rhythm,' tapping her feet. 'I

139

just want to go to a dance, meet a nice boy with dark hair and big blue eyes. Someone to love me. Not too much to ask, is it?'

'Not for a girl like you. You're far too pretty to be stuck in that laundry,' I said.

Marie sighed. 'All I want is to get married, settle down, have a nice little house and kids. Instead we get religion with a capital R shoved down our necks and filthy laundry to do all day, every day.'

When Kitty'd gone I said to Marie, 'Have you never tried to run away one of the days when you were out shopping?'

She sighed. 'I don't have the nerve. I suppose I'm institutionalised by now.'

'What's that?'

'I've got so used to the nuns and the convent that I'm scared of the outside world. You've got to watch it, too, Stella, not to stay there too long or you'll end up thinking the entire universe begins and ends at the Magdalene Laundry.' She sipped her coffee thoughtfully. 'You know some of the girls would do anything to avoid going home.' She lowered her voice. 'Some of them tried to do away with themselves when they got permission to leave, they were so institutionalised. The nuns have been known to listen to their heartbeats in the mornings to make sure they're still alive.'

'That won't happen to me. I can't wait to get out,' I said.

'I wish I felt like that.'

'You're different. You're important to the nuns and they like you.'

'I'm what is known as a consecrated penitent.'

'What's that?'

'Even though I'm a Magdalene I'm one of their "dependable children". I assist them in helping them to maintain the rules. I'm in charge of the newcomers.'

'How did that come about?'

'Well, I was so scared of them in the beginning that I sucked up to them, did all their odd jobs – and did them well. I've been there for five years and they know they can depend on me. It makes life easier,' she said with a meaningful look.

'You must like them,' I said, recalling having glimpsed her here, there and everywhere with them.

Marie grimaced. 'They're all a shower of hypocrites,' she said viciously. 'I'd shoot the lot of them if I had a gun.' But her face broke suddenly into a broad grin of defiance as she said, 'Once, when I first arrived, I was caught trying to escape and I was punished so badly that I never attempted it again.' She spoke lightly but there was scorn in her voice.

'What did they do to you?'

Her voice was hushed as she said, 'Two of the sisters beat me up. By the time they'd finished with me I looked like I'd been run over by a car. They kept a watch on me for a long time after that.' Her eyes were dark and soulful.

'Believe me they left their mark.' She pulled up her sleeves, showed me the white lines on her skin. 'From then on I behaved myself, built up their trust in me.' She laughed a mirthless laugh. 'That's the rock they'll perish on one day,' she added.

Baffled, I looked at her.

'Listen, she said. 'Let me give you a word of advice. 'You have something of the Sleeping Beauty quality about you.'

'Whatdya mean?'

'You're blind to the evil of those nuns. You want to wake up. See what's really going on.' She looked mysterious and important all at once. 'They took my baby and spun me a yarn that it was dead. I knew it was a lie because I saw Father Cronin's housekeeper getting into his car with her. I went mental – screamed the place down. They sent for Father Cronin. I attacked him for taking my baby away from me. He was calm and charming, assuring me that my baby had gone to a good home. You should have heard him shouting at the nuns for their stupidity in letting me see what was going on after I left the parlour. The nuns are afraid of him, you know.'

'What did you do?' I asked, a lump in my throat.

'What *could* I do? They can do what they like, there's no one to check them.' Her face turned scarlet as she said, 'I never found out where my baby was sent – I'll never know.' She bowed her head, lit her cigarette, and blew smoke into the air. 'There's a web of conspiracy around the whole bloody lot of them. They're all rotten to the core.' The sorrow in her face was more than I believed possible in one so full of life. Breaking into a sunny smile, she said, 'Tell me about your fella. Tell me everything.'

'He invited me to his party,' I began. 'Mam made me this beautiful tangerine-coloured frock. She's a dressmaker. After the party, Charles took me home on the back of his motorbike and asked me out on a date. I was mad about him.' I smiled as I recalled flying along on his motorbike, my hair whipping across my face, my arms clasped tight around his waist. It was strange to talk about Charles again. It was like talking to Maeve.

'What happened when you got pregnant?'

'He ran off to work in England.'

'Typical, and you were hoping for a happy ending.'

'He promised to send for me. I knew we couldn't get married. He's a Protestant and he's from a wealthy family. His parents would never have approved of me. But I never expected him to desert me. I thought he was more decent than that.'

'They're all the same,' Marie sighed. 'If I ever leave the Magdalenes I'm not going to bother with fellas. I'm going to lead my own life, earn my own living.'

'Doing what?'

'I want to be a dancer on a stage, like the Royalettes,' she said, a faraway expression in her eyes.

The Angelus bell rang out suddenly, summoning us back to the convent's bleak walls, ending our shared secrets.

Marie said, 'We'll tell the nuns you've got to go back for a check up so we can get out again.'

'Great.'

We said goodbye to Kitty and hurried back.

That night I dreamed that I was waiting at Kingsbridge train station for Charles. Finally the train pulled in, and people streamed off and went in all directions. Charles suddenly appeared. I rushed forward to greet him but he walked straight past me, leaving me standing there. I ran after him, calling him, but he didn't seem to hear me as he disappeared into the crowd. I searched and searched all over for him, but I couldn't find him anywhere.

Fourteen

One day a week later, Sister Perpetua called me out of the Packing Room. 'Stella, you have a visitor,' she said.

'Mam!' I exclaimed joyfully.

'No, your brother. You may spend fifteen minutes with him and then you must get back to work.'

Ciaran – here – on his own! Had he run away? How did he find me? I wondered as I hurried off to the parlour, my heart pounding. I stopped in my tracks when I reached the door and saw a tall young man standing with his back to me, looking out of the window, his hands in the pockets of his good suit. He turned as I came into the room.

'Leo!'

'Stella!' he said, coming forward, brushing his blond quiff of hair back from his forehead. 'How are you?'

'I'm fine,' I said, mortified, knowing I looked a sight. 'Did Mam send you?' I asked hopefully.

'No,' he said reluctantly. 'I'm starting at University College, a pre-med course.'

'Oh! I didn't even know you wanted to be a doctor. You never said so.'

'I didn't think I'd get it. I've had to study so hard that I've almost become a recluse. I thought I'd call in to see you. No one had any news of you and I was getting quite worried.'

'How did you know where to find me?'

'My mother got your address from Father Cooney. She said she wanted to send you a parcel, told me to say that I was your brother or I wouldn't be let in.' He indicated a brown-paper parcel tied with string on the table. 'It's just sweets and cake.'

'That was kind of her, thanks.'

'How are you really?' he asked anxiously, as soon as I closed the door.

'I'm all right, thanks,' I said, determined not to break down and cry in front of him. 'Have you seen my Mam? Is she OK?' I asked him as we sat down.

He nodded. 'She's fine but she doesn't mention your name, so I don't like to ask her about you.' He looked at me with kind, sympathetic eyes. 'I saw Charles yesterday.'

My head shot up. 'Charles!'

'He's back home.'

I could feel myself blush as Leo looked at me. 'I thought you'd want to know.'

'How is he?'

'He's fine. He's been living in Boston, working on

building sites, so he's pretty fit, and brown as a berry from the sun.'

'Was he asking for me?'

'Yes . . .' Leo paused. 'He's worried about you, Stella.'

'Is he? Then why hasn't he got in touch?'

'He's scared and he's confused.' His eyes flicked over me.

'So he sent you to see how I was.'

Leo fixed me with a straightforward look. 'I didn't even tell him I was coming here. He knows he's let you down and he feels terrible about it.'

'So bad that he couldn't drop me a line.' A sob caught in my throat. 'I thought he really cared for me.'

'He did.'

'Until this happened,' I said, looking down at my stomach. 'He treated my pregnancy like a disease, something he might catch if he stuck around. He couldn't even talk about it,' I said. My voice was barely above a whisper.

'He's ashamed of himself for running off,' Leo said. 'He sees himself as a free spirit. He won't let anything tie him down.'

'So why did he come back then?'

Leo leaned forward in his chair. 'His father tracked him down. He would have killed him if he hadn't come back to take his place in college,' Leo went on.

'He got into college?'

'Yes, he's studying architecture in Bolton Street.'

'I might have known he didn't come back because of me.'

'Stella, I'm sorry, I didn't mean to upset you.' Leo hung his head. 'I probably shouldn't have come here.'

'No. It was good of you to come, Leo. I'm glad you did. I haven't seen anyone from home except Father Cooney since I got here. It's not your fault that I'm upset. It's to do with Charles and me.' In the awkward silence the clock ticked loudly. 'I wish that I'd never met him. I was warned off him. But I wouldn't listen.' My voice was shaking; I could hardly draw breath as I spoke.

Leo stood up and came to me. He put his arm around my shoulders in a brotherly way. 'Is there anything I can do, Stella?'

'Tell Mam to come and visit me. I need to see her.'

'I'll call on her as soon as I get home,' promised Leo.

'And don't tell Charles that you saw me like this,' I sniffed.

'I'm not going to say a word to him about you. By the way Maeve sends you all her love. She misses you desperately.'

'Maeve knew you were coming here?'

'Yes, there's a letter from her in your parcel, and Ciaran said to tell you he wants you to come home. I met him at the football match last Sunday; I said I might be seeing you soon, but to keep it a secret.'

'How is he?'

'He's well. He asked me all sorts of awkward questions

about your whereabouts. He wanted to come with me.'

'What did you tell him?'

'That I'd find out if I could bring him with me the next time. That quietened him down. He's getting to be a good little footballer – he's very skilful with the ball, you know.'

'He gets in enough practice.'

All too soon Sister Perpetua opened the door. 'Time to go,' she said, her razor-sharp eyes trained on us both.

I took my parcel and walked with him to the door. 'I'll keep in touch with you,' he promised as we said our goodbyes. He gave me a pat on the arm. 'Just in case anyone's watching, that's what a brother would do, isn't it?' he said.

'Yes.'

'Cheer up, don't let it get you down. You'll be home after you've had the baby won't you?'

'I'll have to see how Mam feels about it.'

'I'll keep in touch,' he promised.

'Thanks, Leo.' I managed to smile as I waved him off.

Later that day Marie cornered me on the corridor and beckoned me outside. 'Was that your fella I saw going into the parlour?' she whispered.

'No, it was his pal, Leo. I've known him all my life.' I told her about the visit.

'Wasn't he courageous, braving it in here, pretending to be your brother. That takes guts, and he's a good-looking lad.' She gave me a quizzical look. 'He must fancy you.'

'Don't be daft, we're friends, that's all.'

I opened the parcel. There was a bag of iced caramels and a bag of Cleeve's toffees, my favourites. Wrapped in greaseproof paper was Leo's mother's home-made fruitcake. There were two packets of biscuits.

Marie and I sat behind the vegetable-garden wall and made pigs of ourselves eating one sweet after another as we thrashed everything out.

'Shame it's not Leo's baby you're having. You wouldn't be in here, that's for sure.'

I said, 'If only I hadn't fallen for Charles.'

'Hindsight is a wonderful thing,' Marie said through a mouthful of toffee.

That evening, I divided the cake and a packet of Kimberly biscuits between the girls in the Ironing Room and Packing Room. Everyone was surprised that the parcel hadn't been confiscated and for a short while I was the most popular girl there.

Fifteen

Coming up to Christmas, the girls decided to put on a concert and Marie got permission from the nuns to do it. She took charge of the auditioning. Some of the girls were very talented. After my audition it was decided that I couldn't sing so I was given the task of painting the scenery with two of the other girls. Marie got costumes from God only knows where. The concert was a great success. The nuns did not attend, of course. They weren't invited. So there was only the other girls, but at least they let us enjoy ourselves for once. It turned out that Bernie had a beautiful voice. She sang 'Silent Night'. There were songs about prisoners and escape, written by girls with total disregard and no fear of the nuns. We howled with laughter and for a short while forgot our loneliness. I knew that I would remember that evening for years to come.

Because of the concert I'd got friendly with most of the girls. Whenever we got the chance, we whispered about boys and love and decent food – and escaping, though we all knew that it was something that could never happen, and that none of the elaborate plans that were hatched in secret would ever come to anything. I could hardly walk, never mind run away, and even if I did manage to escape I had no money, there was nowhere for me to go.

There were Christmas trees in windows. I didn't look at them much because the red, green and yellow lights made my eyes blurry with sadness. There was a crib in the chapel. A big, happy Baby Jesus was placed in it during midnight mass. The priest said in his sermon that Christmas was a time for forgiveness. He said, 'God is watching over us all and he forgives us our sins, as we forgive those who trespass against us'. There and then I forgave Charles for dumping me. I thought about the girls at school who'd been so horrible to me, and forgave them too. I told God that I was sorry for what I'd done and asked him to send me back home. But it didn't work. I didn't feel that I was really forgiven, or that God was listening. I didn't believe that he was watching over me, and even if he was, I didn't think he'd recognise me because I'd changed so much.

By now my baby was fully formed. I could feel its tiny fist fluttering against my ribcage like a trapped butterfly at a window. At night the fluttering and kicking kept me awake. Occasionally the baby jumped inside, making my heart leap with fright.

I was glad when Christmas was over and, out of the blue, I heard from my Auntie Nora. In desperation I'd finally plucked up courage and written to her, telling her of my predicament. She wrote back to Danny's address to say how sorry she was not to have known sooner and that she would visit me as soon as my baby was born. At least not all my family had deserted me.

It snowed all during January. Apart from the Wash House and the Laundry Room, everywhere was cold. Finally the snow melted and the sun shone. The days went by slowly for me because I couldn't do much work. My stomach was swollen up like a balloon and my feet ached. Sister Angela did breathing exercises with me and made me pant alot.

One morning in the Packing Room, a spasm of pain coursed through my body. I closed my eyes and gave in to it, then glanced around to see if anyone had noticed. No one had. There were more pains as the morning wore on. I tried to ignore them until one ripped through my stomach like a jolt of lightning and almost took my breath away. I cried out. One of the girls, Phyllis, came over to me to see what the matter was. At that moment I felt a stream of water gush out of me as if a tap had been turned on inside my body, and I felt my legs weaken. Phyllis caught me before I fell, and lifted me into a standing position. She called two other girls over and between them they hauled me off to the Infirmary, their arms tight around my waist.

Sister Angela took one look at my squirming body and my clenched fists and led me to a bed, declaring that my labour had started. She brought me a cup of sweet tea and came by every so often to check on my progress. As the pains intensified, Sister Angela stayed with me. She held my hand and tried to soothe me, but I turned away from her, calling for Mam through my ragged breath.

'Take deep breaths,' Sister Angela ordered. 'The doctor is on his way.'

Drenched in perspiration I tossed and turned, hardly getting a breath between the spasms. The doctor arrived. In surgical gown and gloves, he examined me. 'You're doing well,' he said. 'Don't worry, I'll tell you what to do.'

I pushed when he told me to, trying to breathe properly. After three hours I was exhausted. My head was throbbing.

Then, when I couldn't push any more, I suddenly I felt something slip between my legs. I looked down to see my baby's head. Minutes later, my baby was born.

'It's a girl,' Sister Angela said, lifting her up and giving her bottom a quick slap.

The baby let out a thin wail and waved her tiny arms and legs in protest. Sister Angela carefully placed her on the weighing scales. 'Five pounds, one ounce,' she declared.

'She's a little underweight, but otherwise perfect,' the doctor said, examining her, pleased with his morning's work.

'Thank you, Doctor,' I said gratefully, as he prepared to leave.

Sister Angela washed her, wrapped her in a tatty white

shawl, and put her in my arms. I couldn't take my eyes off of her as I held her close to me. Her breath tickled my arm as I took in every detail of her face. I couldn't believe that this baby was really mine, yet there was no mistaking her. She had Charles's dark, inquisitive eyes, Mam's dainty nose, Dad's forehead, and Ciaran's mouth. She was beautiful. I held her to me, savouring her newborn smell and the way her mouth opened and closed while her starfish fingers moved restlessly.

'She's hungry,' Sister Angela said, handing me a bottle of formula feed to give her. I put the teat to her lips but her tiny mouth twisted away.

'She won't take it,' Sister.

Sister Angela took her in her expert arms, prized her lips open with the teat, but again she rejected it.

'Stubborn, this one,' she said. 'If she doesn't feed she won't live.'

I held out my arms and took her in them. Automatically, I turned her head towards me and raised it to the level of my breast. Her lips sought out my nipple and fastened on to it, instinctively knowing what to do.

Sister Angela's starched wimple rose with her eyebrows.

'I can't let her starve,' I said resolutely.

'Well, maybe for a day or two, until she get used to the bottle. You're not supposed to breast-feed, child, for your own sake. You'll get too attached to her.'

Sister Angela continued to look doubtful as my baby sucked; her head tipped back, her jaws growing plump with each pull of her lips. Soon her lips stopped sucking and her eyes closed as she rested peacefully against me. I lay quietly gazing at my precious bundle, curled into me as if she'd always been there. As I kissed the top of her silky head, breathing in her sweet baby smell, all the agony of the last nine months seemed to evaporate. 'I'm your Mammy and I'm here to protect you. I won't let anything bad happen to you,' I assured her, showering her with tiny kisses and holding her close to me as my empty promises floated up into the air.

'Finished already?' Sister Angela asked.

'She doesn't want any more.'

Later, Sister Angela weighed her again. 'Her weight's dropped an ounce. She needs to gain quickly or she'll have to go into hospital,' she said, giving her back to me. I changed her to the other side. She sucked half-heartedly for another few minutes. 'Please keep going,' I whispered to her helplessly as I watched her jaws slacking. 'I couldn't bear it if anything were to happen to you.' She must have felt my anxiety. because she sought out my nipple again and drank my worry away.

Sister Angela returned and took her out of my arms.

'Where are you taking her?' I asked, panic-stricken.

'I'm putting her back in her cot so you can rest. She'll need another feed again soon.'

Sister Angela placed her in the wicker basket on wheels and left it beside my bed. I lay on my side and watched my baby covered up in a worn blue cot blanket, afraid to close my eyes for fear she might not be there when I woke up. I held her tiny hand half hoping she would not to take her feed. 'If you die, I want to die with you and go to heaven with you,' I whispered before I fell asleep, holding her tiny hand in mine.

Her whimper woke me. I scrambled out of bed, lifted her into my arms. Back in bed I felt the grip of her gums as she latched on to me immediately. 'You are a clever girl,' I said, touching her cheek, stroking her silky head, never taking my eyes off of her as she fed. This helpless little creature was my very own flesh and blood, and depended on me for everything. The enormity of this realisation scared me. I bit down hard on my lip to fight the intense fear that took hold of me. I was too young for all this responsibility.

When she finished I raised her in my arms. 'Clever girl,' I said, kissing her cheek. It was as soft as a gossamer wing. 'I'm not alone in this world any more. I'll never be alone again now that I have you.' I lay there wishing we could stay like that for ever and ever.

Sixteen

One morning, a few days later, I woke up to see Father Cooney standing over me. My heart leaped with shock and instinctively I glanced towards the cot. My baby was fast asleep.

'Hello Stella,' Father Cooney said pleasantly. 'How are you?'

'I'm fine.'

What did he want? Had he come to take my baby from me? If so, how could I stop him?

'You have a lovely baby, thank God,' he said.

'Yes.' Then with all the courage I could muster and my heart pounding, I said, 'Have you come to take her away?'

He shook his head. 'I've come to baptise her. I hear she's a little on the weak side.'

'She's not going to die, is she?' I said, my heart in my mouth.

'Of course not. But I promised your mam I'd come and baptise her.'

Tears stung my eyes at the mention of my mam. 'She knows I had my baby?'

'Yes, she's relieved that it's all over.'

'Is she coming to see us?' I asked, wanting her there more than I had ever wanted anything in my life.

'I don't think so . . . but she's very concerned about you.'

'How's Ciaran? Does he know?' It was strange asking Father Cooney about my own family.

'Ah no, he's a bit on the young side for that kind of information, but he's getting on fine.'

'I don't suppose I'll be able to go home.'

'I don't see why not, once the baby's been given up for adoption.'

'I'm not giving her up, I'm keeping her, Father.'

Father Cooney put his hand to his ear as if he'd misheard me.

'I've thought about it and I've decided to keep her,' I repeated.

'I thought that's what you said.' He looked bewildered.

'You could talk to Mam. A word from you will make it all right. All I want is for us to live together again, like a family.' I could hear the longing for that wish to be granted in my voice.

'But you have no way of supporting the child. Neither has your mother. Surely you realise that she can barely make ends meet as it is.'

'I'll leave school, get a job. We won't be a burden.'

'Your mother is just about able to cope with Ciaran, Stella, never mind a brand-new baby.'

I looked at him right between the eyes. 'I'll think of some way of keeping her.'

He regarded me with distaste. I'm very disappointed in you. I thought you were willing to put the past behind you and start afresh, make amends to your mother for all the heartbreak you've caused her.'

'Not if it means giving up my baby.' I raised my chin defiantly.

'You'll see sense and change your mind.'

'No I won't, you should never have brought me here in the first place.'

Father Cooney's face clouded over. In a cracked voice he said, 'This is your own doing, Stella, it's your own fault.'

Sister Angela came into the room with the christening accoutrements. I looked from one to the other with an overwhelming sense of defeat. Though not a single word passed between them I knew I would have no say in my baby's future.

'Can Marie be her godmother?' I asked Sister Angela.

'Certainly, I'll send for her.' She went off as Father Cooney, ignoring me, put on his mass robes. Sister Angela returned with Marie and a jug of water that she handed to Father Cooney. Marie took the baby and held her over an old wash basin.

'What is this child's name?' Father Cooney asked formally.

'Holly,' I said with assurance.

'That's not a Christian name.'

'It's after Buddy Holly.'

Father Cooney looked as if he might drop the jug of water.

'It's a lovely name,' Marie said quickly. 'It's . . . different.'

'It's of no consequence,' Sister Angela said gently. 'The name will be changed by its adoptive parents.'

'She'll be Holly for the length of time that I have her, and I'd like to have Eileen as her second name, after my mother,' I said.

Father Cooney performed the ceremony reluctantly, saying, 'I baptise you, Holly Eileen Wood,' and pouring half the jug of freezing-cold water over her head on purpose to make her roar.

'That'll open up her lungs, do her all the good in the world,' Sister Angela said when she saw my stricken face.

As soon as it was over Father Cooney left without another word to me, fully satisfied that he'd secured another soul for God and fulfilled Mam's wishes at the same time.

After had I fed her, I lay her down in her cot and covered her with the threadbare blankets that hundreds of Magdalene babies before her had slept under. Her mouth worked as her eyes closed. Soon she was asleep.

'You're a film star already with a name like that, beautiful baby,' Marie smiled, handing me a soft pink teddy bear. 'Every little girl needs a teddy to cuddle.' She placed it beside Holly, who gave a shuddering sigh as Marie leaned over her.

'Where did you get that?'

'Ask no questions, you'll be told no lies,' she laughed.

During the next few days Holly gained one pound in weight. I was delighted but Sister Angela said it wasn't enough. 'She's not fit to go out yet. You'll have her another week or two, until she's stronger.'

I was overjoyed. After each feed I would hold her for a long time, talking to her, and savouring her fresh smell of milk and baby powder. Reluctantly, I would return her to her cot, pull the blankets up to her ear to make sure she was warm, then lie watching her head moving back and forth, her thumb trying to find her mouth. Only when she was settled comfortably would I let myself fall asleep.

When she cried I would lift her out of her cot. Red-faced and ravenous, she made faint smacking noises as she fed. But each time she tired quickly and her jaws would slacken. I would lean over her trying to encourage her to drink more. She would grasp my finger tightly and I vowed then that I would never let her go because she was mine. I had been given this child to take care of her. Being a mother was an important job and it was important that I should do it.

There would be problems. That I knew. We'd be poor for a start, but we'd manage. We wouldn't go back to

Knocknacree. I'd get a live-in job somewhere and work hard. We'd be very happy together, sharing everything. That was enough to start with. Of course I'd have to tell the nuns what I planned. They would try to fight me. But surely I'd win out in the end. We'd cope. I firmly believed all of this because I needed to. I loved Holly as fiercely as any mother could love her baby. I couldn't imagine being without her. It was unthinkable.

Auntie Nora kept her promise. One morning she came quickly into my cell in a dazzle of red coat and scarf to match. 'Stella!' she cried, her voice shattering the silence as she bounced towards me in a flurry of parcels, her high heels clicking on the wooden floor, sunlight lifting up her spun-gold frizzy hair, her happy, smiling face lighting up the place.

'Auntie Nora!' I gasped in thrilled shock.

Her arms enfolded me like a warm, protective shawl. Squeezing me to her lavender-scented bosom in a tight embrace, she asked, 'And how are you?'

'I'm so glad to see you,' I said, breathlessly, tears rolling down my cheeks.

'Ah, hush there, love. I'm here now.' Gently, she stroked my hair. 'It's terrible what happened to you, and you only a child yourself. You've been through the mill.' She went to the cot, leaned towards it. 'Look at this beautiful baby. Isn't she only gorgeous? Hello darling,' she cooed softly to Holly.

'Would you like to hold her?' I sniffed.

She reached out and lifted Holly up in her arms. Holly leaned into her shoulder. 'You're a little beauty,' she said to her, holding her firmly in the crook of her arm. 'Light as a feather too. Isn't your Mammy a clever girl to have produced such a smashing baby.'

'Her name is Holly. She's not gaining enough weight, that's why I'm allowed to feed her myself,' I said in a wobbly voice.

Holly whimpered. 'Poor little pet.' Auntie Nora rocked her to and fro, her bracelets jangling. Holly looked at up at her. 'When it comes to babies I always know what to do,' Auntie Nora said delightedly. 'The twins gave me a good training. They were a holy fright to rear.'

'I want to keep her.' The lump in my throat was so big that I could hardly speak.

'I don't blame you. I would too if she were mine.'

Sister Perpetua appeared in the doorway. Auntie Nora faced her. 'Isn't she a lovely baby, Sister.'

Sister Perpetua nodded her head. 'A bit on the small side, but she's coming on nicely.'

Auntie Nora put Holly into my arms. 'Look at that, she's a born mother.'

Lips pursed, Sister Perpetua sniffed. 'We don't encourage the mothers to become attached to the child. It only makes matter worse in the long run.'

'But Stella wants to keep her,' Auntie Nora said bluntly.

'There's no possibility of that. The baby is delicate, she needs a good home and caring parents to look after her properly.'

'Not surprising she's delicate. It's nothing short of a miracle that she's any way normal, considering Stella's lack of nutrition and proper care during her pregnancy.' Auntie Nora's voice rose in anger.

Sister Perpetua glared at her. 'How dare you to speak to me like that! This baby has parents and a good home to go to, something that Star here could never provide for her.'

Auntie Nora glared right back at her. 'Star! Who's Star?' she asked, looking around, puzzled.

'That's my name in here,' I said, meekly.

Auntie Nora twirled around to me. 'They changed your name?'

'Yes.' I kept my eyes downcast.

She turned back to Sister Perpetua. 'I've heard terrible stories about the treatment of the girls in this place and about the babies that are sent out from here too, some as far away as America, and without the mother's permission. We won't have that, Sister.'

Gripped by sudden panic, I sucked in my breath and folded Holly into me.

'I can assure you that this baby is being placed with a good Irish Catholic family,' said the furious nun. 'You should be grateful that there are adoptive parents who are willing to give her the best of everything.'

Auntie Nora's eyebrows arched as she scanned Sister Perpetua's angry face. She said, in slightly milder vein, 'Grateful is it? *They* should be grateful. I'll want to know every detail of Holly's progress from now on.'

Sister Perpetua shifted her weight from one foot to the other, 'That's not part of our policy.'

'Then you'd better make it your policy or there'll be trouble.'

'I think you should leave.' Sister Perpetua was angrier than I'd ever seen her but she didn't frighten Auntie Nora.

'Not until I've had a proper talk with my niece. Now, I didn't come here to start a fight, but that's what you'll get if you try to stop me.' Auntie Nora didn't give Sister time to reply. 'I'd like a word with Stella in private, if you wouldn't mind.'

Tall and wide, she stood between fear and me. Sister Perpetua turned and left the room, having no argument to counter that remark.

Auntie Nora sat down on the bed beside me. She reached for my hand and said, 'I'm going to make sure that Holly is well cared for. I won't let anyone harm a hair of her head, or yours either. If only I'd known you were here sooner I'd have been in to throw my weight around long ago, and God knows there's enough of it,' she laughed.

'Thanks, I'm really grateful. Mam hasn't been in touch with me at all,' I told her.

She sighed. 'I know what your Mam's like. She can be very stubborn. Maybe when I write and tell her that Holly has a great look of her she might have a change of heart.'

I shook my head. 'She's too scared of what the neighbours will think and say.'

'To hell with the neighbours. I don't know why she's so concerned about them. Let them think what they want to think, that's what I always say.' She patted my hand. 'You leave your Mam to me. I'll get her to see sense. But you'll have to be patient. It might take a while.'

We talked on. Auntie Nora didn't laugh at me when I told her about my hopes and dreams for the future. She understood my plight and even praised me for my bravery in facing up to the 'awful nuns.' I felt safe with her on my side.

'Now is there anything you want me to get for you?'

'No, thank you. How's Uncle Billy?' I'd forgotten to ask about him in all the excitement.

'He's his usual grumpy self, but otherwise fine.' She put her arms around me and kissed me on the cheek, promising she'd be back. She blew Holly a kiss and left, waving as she went.

I knew she wouldn't be back. Sister Perpetua would make sure of that.

Over the next week Holly gained another pound in weight, and I was getting stronger too. Sister Angela was pleased with our progress. Being allowed to have Holly with me and feed her myself was surely a sign that the nuns were having a change of heart about having her adopted. Perhaps we would be allowed into the outside world to make a life of our own after all.

Seventeen

Early one morning I woke up to what I thought was the sound of Holly's sucking noises. As I rose to take her out of her basket I made out the outline of Marie sitting at the end of my bed.

'Marie! What are you doing here? What's up? Is Mam sick? Is Ciaran all right?'

She clasped my hand. 'It's Holly. They've taken her away, love.'

I leaped out of bed. The cot was empty. 'No!' I cried. Marie put her arms around me, and held me tight. 'When?' I whispered, my hands trembling.

'In the night.'

'Where have they taken her?'

'I don't know.'

'They can't take my baby away from me without a word,' I wailed.

'They did.'

Sister Angela came rushing in when she heard the commotion. I ran to her, grabbed her veil. 'Where's Holly?' I shouted at her.

'Calm down, Star,' she said, shocked.

'Not until you tell me where she is.' I kept hold of her veil as she tried to back away from me, and would have pulled it off her head if Marie hadn't caught my arms and held them behind my back. She advised Sister Angela to go, assuring her that she would take care of me, and Sister Angela was only too glad to oblige.

When she'd gone, Marie made me take slow, deep breaths. 'You're not alone, I'll stay with you and help you,' she said.

As soon as I was calmer, Marie helped me back into bed. I eventually fell asleep and dreamed of Holly, and woke up to face the emptiness. Though the cot was gone the cell contained her as if she was still there. Her warmth enveloped me. I could smell her sweetbaby smell, feel her soft downy head, see her honey-coloured skin. Everywhere was full of her; the prints of her mouth were on her bib, the dress with the smocking that Auntie Nora had brought her was still hanging on the back of the door. It moved in the breeze from the window as if she was in it. Her tiny white hairbrush lay on the bedside locker, still in its plastic wrapping. But it was the stillness that held her the most, as if she was clinging to the room.

The horror of being without her hit me so suddenly that I had to sit up. Caught in a stranglehold of fear and hopelessness, I could barely breathe with the loneliness. A dull ache started in my head and moved to my heart.

Sister Angela brought me a mug of tea and a slice of

toast. 'You'll soon be all right,' she said. I ignored her and kept my eyes fixed on the blowing trees outside. Soon those trees would be covered in leaves and Holly would be living in a stranger's home, being fed by an unknown woman she would learn to call Mother. That thought was worse than the worst nightmare I'd ever had.

I was still gazing out of the window, stifled by the dead institutional air and my own inability to get Holly back when Marie returned. 'I'm going out of my mind,' I told her.

'No you're not, you only think that,' she consoled.

'I'm not staying here. I'm going, my mind's made up,' I said. 'I won't let them get away with this.'

Marie blinked at me. 'But where to?'

'I'll go to Auntie Nora. She'll help me get Holly back.'

'Even if you were to get her back, it would be a terrible struggle trying to bring her up on your own,' Marie warned. 'You've no training for anything. You'd end up on a factory floor where they'd exploit you.'

'I don't care, I can't take any more of this place.' Hatred for the nuns welled up inside me.

'And you may never find a man who is willing to take Holly on.' Marie's tone made me angry. I looked at her. 'I'm only putting the facts to you so you know what you're letting yourself in for. I mean, how can you look after her and work at the same time?'

'Auntie Nora will help me, I know she will. Don't try and stop me.'

'I'm not going to try and stop you,' Marie said. 'I'm going to help you.'

I regarded her. 'Do you mean that?'

'Yes.'

'Do you know where they've taken Holly?' I asked her cautiously.

'No, but I might be able to find out.' She put her finger to her lips. 'You must promise me that you'll be patient and not make any more fuss.'

'I promise.'

Marie went off. She was gone for what seemed a long time. When she returned she told me that Holly was still in the convent. 'She's in the nuns' quarters, ready to go out first thing in the morning.'

I jumped out of bed. I wanted to burst in and get her back right there and then. Marie's outstretched arms stopped me. 'You can't do anything now, it's getting dark outside. Wait until the morning.' She led me back to bed. 'We have to make a plan.'

Whispering together, we planned, plotted and schemed. We agreed that first thing in the morning, while the nuns were at mass, I would take Holly and make my escape. Marie would smuggle out a few clothes for her and then she would deny any knowledge of my escape to the nuns. 'They'll have the police out looking for you, so you'd better be careful. Keep an eye out for the cops, no matter where you are.' I assured her that I would.

After she'd gone I lay awake for a long time, filled with

excitement at the thought of seeing Holly again. I imagined the pandemonium in the convent when it was discovered that we'd gone. I could see all of the nuns blustering around. Reverend Mother would lash out at Sister Angela saying, 'Why didn't one of you keep a closer eye on her?' Sister Angela would say apologetically, 'I did, and she didn't look as if she was going anywhere.' Sister Perpetua would say, 'I didn't think she had it in her.' Sister Michael, who echoed Sister Perpetua's views at all times, would nod in agreement. I couldn't think about it too much for fear I might lose my nerve. Instead I thought of Auntie Nora's happy, smiling face at the sight of us. Not that I would expect too much of her. Just a roof over my head until I got myself organised. I would look after my own daughter. All I had to do was get a job and a bed-sitting room.

As soon as it was daylight I got up, pulled the curtains, and looked out of the window. Clouds hung over the rooftops and chimneys. Snowflakes floated around weightlessly, disappearing into the sludge on the ground like ghosts.

I dressed quickly, putting a change of clothes for Holly and some nappies in a carrier bag. I sneaked downstairs as soon as I heard the convent bell chime for mass. Marie was waiting for me at the well of the staircase. I gave the carrier bag to her, then tiptoed along the chapel corridor and hid behind the chapel door, watching the community and the girls go into mass. As soon as the prayers floated out of the chapel, I crossed the corridor and was making my way silently to the parlour when Sister Luke appeared from nowhere.

I jumped back.

'Where are you going, child?' she asked, her hunched-up body blocking my path, her black habit stark against the white wall.

'Toilet, Sister, I'm bursting,' I said, sure that my guilt was obvious.

'Well, hurry back or you'll be late,' she said, and went on her way. I walked swiftly on, then doubled back and sneaked down to the parlour.

Just as Marie had said, a Moses basket sat in the corner and inside it Holly was fast asleep. My palms sweating, I lifted her up. She began to whimper. 'Don't cry, darling, Mammy's here,' I whispered to her, wrapping her up in the snow-white shawl that was in the Moses basket.

My heart was pounding as we stole back along the corridor, past the chapel and over to the back door of the laundry, where Marie was waiting with the keys to open it. Silently, she handed me a coat. I put it on, hid Holly inside it as Marie unlocked the door. With shaking legs I stepped outside.

Marie handed me a big shopping basket. 'You can put Holly in that if your arms get tired.'

'Thanks, and don't worry about me, I'll be fine,' I assured her.

'This is it then.' Tears shone in her eyes.

I hugged her. 'I'll see you again. I'll come back for you one day and take you away from all this,' I promised.

She gave me a little red purse. 'There's a couple of quid in there for your train fare. Mind yourself.'

'Thanks.'

With a shaky smile Marie whispered, 'Go, and be safe, I'll keep nix for you.'

I didn't have time to be sad about leaving my friend as I sneaked down by the side of the shrubbery and past the big Crucifixion statue, looking left and right to make sure there was no about, before I finally stepped out through the side gate on to the main road. Dizzy with freedom I walked as fast as I could, holding Holly tightly and taking deep breaths to calm myself as I left the convent railings behind. I crossed the road to the little park I'd seen from my window and disappeared into the trees, sidestepping clumps of bushes and spiky nettles that sprouted up like an army of enemies. I pushed my way through the tangled wilderness, clinging tightly to Holly as I went. I hid behind a tree as two men passed by.

Out on the open road, away from the convent, I went to the bus depot and got the bus to Booterstown train station, following Marie's instructions all the way. There I bought a train ticket to Bray. The station was quiet, only a couple of people waiting for the train. No one took any notice of me as I sat waiting. Holly stirred, then whimpered. I walked up and down the platform with her until the train arrived.

Most of the carriages were empty. As soon as I got into one I fed Holly. The soothing, rocking motion sent her off to sleep. I gazed out of the window at the stillness of the desolate grey sea, and felt an overwhelming sense of relief, excitement and nerves. No more laundry, no more nuns! No more fear of the daily tortures or cracks on the knuckles with hard rosary beads; no more lashes from leather belts. But the exhilaration was soon followed by a growing sense of fear at the thought of entering a strange world. I reminded myself that I was going to my good, kind Auntie Nora, the nicest person in the world.

Mam, Dad, Ciaran and I used to spend part of our summer holidays with Auntie Nora and Uncle Billy. Our big cousins, Jack and Brian (the twins), would take us to the amusements on the seafront. We would ride in the ghost trains, swirl round on the hobbyhorses, our tummies churning from too much candyfloss and ice cream. In the evenings we would play hide and seek in the woods and chase each other home in the dark. After tea round the big kitchen table Dad would go to the pub with Uncle Billy, and Brian and Jack would tell us frightening tales of ghosts in haunted houses. But Jack and Brian grew up and moved away and we finally stopped going on holiday to Bray when Dad lost his job.

★ ★ ★

At Bray station the ticket man took my ticket. I walked quickly along the promenade past big ancient-looking houses and shuttered kiosks, a bar and a run-down hotel – all of which I recognised – and turned right up the hill, sure of my way. I got confused as I passed a new housing estate where all the houses looked the same. Soon, my feet were aching and my heart was thumping as I tried to keep track of the way. Holly was getting heavier with each step. Eventually, I passed a familiar-looking corner shop and knew that I was in the vicinity of Auntie Nora's house.

As soon as I saw the neat line of hedge and the white semi-detached house behind it, I recognised it. My heart beat fast as I opened the gate with 'The Elms' written on it. Resolutely, I walked up the path and rang the bell, forcing myself to breathe slowly as I pulled my coat over Holly and waited.

Uncle Billy answered the door. A small, bustling man with tight curly hair, he looked startled to see me. 'Stella! What a surprise! What brings you here?' he asked.

'Hello Uncle Billy,' I said, hesitantly. 'I came to see Auntie Nora.'

She's out just now, I'm afraid, love,' he told me. 'But come in, I'll make a brew. She won't be long.

I followed him into the kitchen and I told him that I'd left the convent and needed somewhere to stay with Holly. He eyed her nervously as she slept, huddled up inside my coat.

'So, how long are you planning on staying?' he asked when I'd finished.

'Just 'til I get fixed up in a job,' I said, stepping across the familiar linoleum floor of their old-fashioned kitchen.

Uncle Billy looked uncomfortable but his tone was friendly. 'Nora won't be long. Make yourself at home.' He left me there to wait. So I took Holly to the bathroom, where I fed and changed her.

When I finally heard the scrape of her key in the lock, I leaped up and practically fell into her arms with relief.

'Stella, love, what happened?' she asked, surprised and delighted to see me.

I told her the whole story too.

'Of course you can stay here,' she said. 'You poor thing, you look so tired and you must be starving.' She put the kettle on for a cup of tea, then cooked rashers, eggs and fried potatoes for our dinner. Holding Holly while I ate, Auntie Nora relayed my tale of woe to Uncle Billy, saying indignantly to me. 'Why shouldn't you keep your own baby. You're worth so much more than being a skivvy for them nuns. What a cheek they have.'

'I'm sorry, but haven't you missed an important point here, Nora,' Uncle Billy broke in with his mouth half full.

'What?' Auntie Nora asked.

'Isn't it illegal for Stella to snatch the baby and walk out just like that? Won't the nuns and the adoptive parents be going frantic wondering where the baby's gone?' he asked, his eyes fixed on me.

'Holly is Stella's baby, Billy,' Auntie Nora said. 'She hasn't signed any papers, have you, love?'

'No, I haven't.'

'Well then, they've no rights, so you've nothing to worry about. This isn't a Trade Union matter you're dealing with,' she admonished him. 'We're talking about Stella's rights to her own child.'

'Well, don't the nuns have rights too?' he said.

'Phst. They made a slave of her,' Auntie Nora said.

'Fine,' said Uncle Billy, 'but I want to make it clear that I'm not getting involved if the cops come looking for you, Stella, understand? You're here at your own risk.'

My jaw dropped. I'd psyched myself up into thinking that everything was going to be all right once I got to Auntie Nora's. I'd forgotten how testy Uncle Billy could be, with his Trade Union ideals. All of a sudden a vision of the laundry rose in front of me, Uncle Billy marching me through its doors. As soon as the meal was over I excused myself and went upstairs to the back bedroom. Auntie Nora followed.

'Don't mind Billy, I'll talk him round. You'll be comfortable here,' she said, getting sheets out of the hot press, quickly making the bed.

It was an airy room with a long window that looked out over the back garden and woods to the side of Bray Head. The fact that I had a room of my own with a lavatory next door to it was heaven to me. Being able to walk around without having to ask permission was bliss. The only blot on my landscape was Uncle Billy. I'd need to watch out for him. Auntie Nora put a drawer from her chest of drawers by my bed for Holly to sleep in. She used a pillow for a mattress and doubled a small rug to cover her. She gave me shampoo, soap and a towel, then tore up a couple of old towels for extra nappies. I gave Holly her night feed, changed her, and put her in the drawer for the night. Finally, exhausted, I went to bed too.

The mattress was soft, the sheets and pillows crisp. Suspended on a cloud of comfort I slept soundly. Holly cried in the night. I fed and changed her again, hoping that she wouldn't wake up the household. After only a couple of hours she cried again. I walked her up and down the room rocking her, praying that she wouldn't wake up Uncle Billy. Eventually, she dropped off to sleep in my arms.

I woke up to a bright day. Everywhere was still and quiet. My first thoughts were of the nuns. By now they'd have the police out looking for me. The nuns would surely have got in touch with Mam and worried the life out of her.

As soon as Holly woke up I fed her so that she wouldn't start crying. Watching the sun streaming through the window, I nestled her into me and explained to her that we'd got to make this great escape work. 'I don't believe your daddy will ever come to find us,' I told her sadly. 'It's time I forgot about him. I've to get a job quickly and get out from under Uncle Billy's feet, because he doesn't really want us around.' Holly gave me a windy smile.

Auntie Nora was in the kitchen when we went downstairs.

'I hope Holly didn't disturb you in the night. She kept waking up,' I said.

'No, I didn't hear a sound. We'll buy her a carrycot in the second-hand shop this morning.'

I bathed Holly in the sink, dressed her in the only clean clothes she possessed, and put her in Uncle Billy's armchair. She fell asleep instantly. Uncle Billy came downstairs, said good morning and ate his breakfast in silence while Auntie Nora planned our shopping trip to buy baby things. We left him scowling into his tea and set out for the town.

Auntie Nora bought nappies, plastic pants, romper suits, bibs, matinée coats, baby sheets, and blankets – even a plastic bucket. She even bought me a pretty frock in bright colours as a treat.

'I never realised how many things a baby needs,' I said, as I pushed the parcels home in the neat, blue second-hand pram.

Uncle Billy gave me a look that would curdle milk as he surveyed the shopping bags. He was about to make a comment, but a look from Auntie Nora stopped him in his tracks.

I was putting Holly to bed in her new carrycot when the doorbell rang. She began to whimper. 'Shh,' I soothed her. We've got to keep quietly to ourselves. We don't want to upset Uncle Billy, coming and going in his house.'

'Stella!' Uncle Billy called up the stairs.

I lay Holly in her cot and went downstairs to see Leo standing on the doorstep, a hostile Uncle Billy blocking the entrance.

'Leo?'

Uncle Billy sighed and stepped aside and let him in.

Blushing, Leo came into the hallway. 'Stella, the cops have been going round Knocknacree making enquiries about you. Your Mam thinks that you might have come here. She's very worried about you. She sent me to tell you to go back to the laundry.'

'I knew it,' Uncle Billy said, almost with glee. 'I told you this would happen. What are we going to do?'

'Calm down,' Auntie Nora said, taking Leo into the kitchen. She made tea and listened while he gave a full account of the trauma in Knocknacree.

'Tell Stella's Mam that when you got here Stella had already left for England. If she tells that to the cops they'll drop the search,' she advised.

'Good idea. I'll phone my mother right away. She'll give her the news,' Leo said.

Uncle Billy looked unhappy about the plan. But he stayed out of the conversation, thankfully. Then as soon as

Leo left I said to him, 'You won't have to worry about keeping us for long, I'm going to get a job.'

'Doing what, might I ask?' he enquired sarcastically.

'Well, I was working in Irene's café part-time and I know how to waitress.'

'You'll have no trouble getting a job in a café coming up to the summer,' Auntie Nora said.

'The summer season's a long way off,' Uncle Billy chimed in.

'You could try the café at the railway station. It's always busy,' Auntie Nora suggested.

'And who'll mind your baby if you do get work?'

'I will,' Auntie Nora said. 'I've been thinking of finding a little job and looking after Holly will do nicely for the time being.'

'You'll be paying her?' Uncle Billy asked me.

'Yes,' I said.

'And you'll be giving us something towards your keep?'

'Of course I will.'

'That's all right then.' He perked up immediately.

'Don't take any notice of him,' Auntie Nora said as soon as he'd left the kitchen. 'He's out of sorts with the petrol strike. Doesn't know what to be doing with himself when he's not driving his bus all day.'

Eighteen

The next day I put on my new frock, used some of Auntie Nora's creme puff powder and lipstick to look more grown up, and left her babysitting while I went off went job-hunting.

The town was busy with early-morning shoppers. Passing the café at the station, I saw a notice in the window. It said:

WAITRESS WANTED PART TIME.
GOOD WAGES PLUS TIPS.

I braced myself, pushed the door open and walked in bravely. The sweet smell of coffee made me feel at home.

'What can I get you?' a girl with short black hair asked me from behind the counter.

I cleared my throat. 'It's about your ad in the window; I'd like the job,' I said, pointing to the notice.

She looked me up and down. 'What's your name?'

'Stella Wood.'

'I'll go and get the manager. Wait there.'

She disappeared. I stood nervously looking around at the red-topped plastic tables. The juke box in the corner was playing 'It Doesn't Matter Any More' and thoughts of Charles suddenly flooded through me. I had to banish them quickly and concentrate hard on the moment.

The girl returned, followed by a tall, broad-shouldered man with slicked-back hair and a blustery manner.

'This is the girl who wants the job,' she said, pointing to me.

'Hello, I'm Dave.' He led me to a table. 'Sit down,' he said, looking hard at me. 'How old are you?' he asked.

'Seventeen,' I lied.

'Have you worked as a waitress before?'

'Yes. I had a part-time job in a café while I was at school.'

'Any references?'

I was about to give the name of the café at home but stopped myself in the nick of time. 'No, but I can get one. And I know how to work that new coffee machine.'

Dave looked slightly impressed. But his tone was flat. 'We open early, close late,' he said. 'You'd be working shift hours.'

'That wouldn't be a problem,' I assured him.

'You've got to be smart to work in a place like this, we get all sorts,' he said.

'Of course. And I'm good with people – I'm used to hard work too.'

'So I see.' His eyes were on my red hands and shredded nails. 'It gets a bit hectic here at times. You'd be waiting tables and serving at the counter all at the same time. Could you handle that?'

I hesitated only for a split second. 'Yes.'

'Do you live nearby?'

'Yes.'

He looked me up and down. 'Your wages would be five pounds a week. Of course you'll get tips as well and maybe a pay rise when you've proved your worth.'

'Sounds great,' I said enthusiastically.

'The uniform's black with a white apron, as you can see. Can you start tomorrow? Week's trial?'

I blinked in surprise. 'Yes. Thanks. I'm really grateful.'

He laughed. 'Don't mention it. I'm not doing you any favours. Like I said, you'll be working hard.' He rose. 'See you tomorrow morning then, eight o'clock sharp.'

As I was leaving he called me back, opening the till and handing me two pounds, ten shillings. 'That's an advance on your wages. You'll get a plain black dress in Traynor's and wear more make-up. I don't want to be had up for cradle-snatching.'

Relieved, I went to Traynor's to buy the dress, visualising Dave giving orders and taking no slack from anyone.

'He wants you to start tomorrow!' Auntie Nora exclaimed when I got back.

'Very unsociable hours,' Uncle Billy said.

Auntie Nora said. 'Now, you're not to worry. I'm here for Holly, she'll be safe with me, but you'll have to wean her on to the bottle. I'll buy one first thing in the morning.'

My mouth went dry as it dawned on me how much I was going to miss her. But it was a start in the right direction for both of us. 'Now I can save up for a place of my own,' I said to Uncle Billy.

'Good,' he said.

'There's no rush,' Auntie Nora said.

But, 'The sooner the better,' Uncle Billy muttered under his breath.

At the café the next morning, I donned my apron and nervously took the breakfast orders. Everyone was friendly. The girls in the kitchen greeted me with a cheery hello. Even the delivery man welcomed me. Theresa, the girl I'd met the previous day, surveyed me from her perch behind the till and said, 'Don't be scared, you'll be all right when you've been round the tables a couple of times.' She was right. By eleven o'clock the café was humming and I was buzzing around serving endless cups of coffee.

At lunchtime I raced around taking orders for egg, bacon and chips, serving, clearing – perspiration trickling down my back, cold against my skin.

Theresa was busy on the cash register all day so I had to guess at the names of the various types of pastries in the display cabinet, or get the customer to point them out to me. I was doing this when I had a strong instinct that I was being watched. When I turned away from my customer, I locked eyes with a woman in a beige coat who was sitting alone and staring at me. 'Don't I know you from somewhere?' she said, tapping her spoon on her saucer thoughtfully.

'I don't think so,' I said, and quickly moved away from the counter to take another order from two well-dressed ladies with shopping baskets. But I was aware that all the time the woman had her eyes on me. I imagined my photograph on a missing-person's poster all over the city being viewed by every passer-by, my details in big writing beneath it.

Stella Wood, five foot eight, slim with red shoulder-length hair, temper to match, and blue eyes; wearing a brown overcoat, pink scarf; last seen in the Bray area.

The nuns won't stop until they've tracked me down, I thought miserably.

As the day went on I was so busy serving, clearing the tables, stacking the dirty crockery in the kitchen in the back, that my fear was forgotten in the rush. By four o'clock I was beginning to settle in, and as I was leaving Dave smiled at me. 'Good work, Stella,' he said, pleased with my day's work.

I got back to Auntie Nora's exhausted, ready for

nothing except bed and sleep. Auntie Nora was waiting for me with Holly in her arms. 'She's fed and ready for bed. She took to the bottle no bother. She's as good as gold,' she said, handing her over to me. 'How did you get on?' she asked. 'Did you like it?'

'It was busy, the time flew by,' I said, and yawned. 'I'll take over Holly from here. Thanks, Auntie Nora.' I took Holly upstairs to feed her, glad of some time alone with her. 'I missed you my lovely baby,' I told her as suckled contentedly.

'You look exhausted; have a hot bath, you'll feel better,' Auntie Nora said when I returned to the kitchen.

I lay in the bath for ages, soaking away the aches and pains. Afterwards, over a cup of tea I told Auntie Nora all about the staff and customers.

'Maybe you're doing too much, too soon,' she said. 'I'm sure you could find an easier job than that one if you looked around.'

'No, it's fine. I like it,' I said.

Next morning I dragged myself out of bed, bleary-eyed and stiff all over, every limb aching. I fed Holly and took her downstairs. After breakfast Auntie Nora took her over to let me get ready for work.

Before the café got busy Dave taught me the names of the different cakes and pastries. 'You're a good worker, the best we've had here for a long time,' he said. His words of encouragement made me work even harder.

At lunchtime a man and a woman came in, holding hands. There was a smile on the man's face as the woman talked. I couldn't take my eyes off them, they looked so happy. Charles's face swam before me. We'd been happy together like that once. How had it all gone so wrong?

Each day a steady stream of customers came into the café. Each night, stiff and tired, my feet sore, my ankles swollen, I would feed Holly and listen as Auntie Nora went over the day's events with her.

By the end of the first week the job was getting easier. I gave Auntie Nora half my wages for our keep and some extra for minding Holly. She didn't want to take it, but I insisted on it.

The following week I was on the late shift, which meant that I had the daytime to spend with Holly. I fed her, played with her, took her for a walks in the afternoons.

One night Leo called into the café, to assure me that everything was back to normal at home. 'Everyone thinks you're in England,' he said as I served him with a cup of coffee. I couldn't help thinking that surely Mam must be worried about me knowing I wasn't with Dad.

Back at the counter, Theresa nudged me. 'Who's your friend?' she asked.

'He's a pal from home.'

She gave me a little secret smile. 'You can go early if you like, we're not busy,' she said.

'Are you sure?'

'Of course,' she said looking around. 'It's nearly closing and Dave's not here. I can clear up on my own.'

'You seem to be coping well,' Leo said when we got outside.

'Yes, it's not so bad. How's life treating you?' I asked him.

'Good, I've got a summer job – delivery man for Savage Sweets. The south side of the city is my area. Charles's mother organised it for me.'

'That's terrific.'

'I feel I'm out of my depth in the big smoke though – don't know my way round yet.'

'You'll soon learn.'

'How's Holly?'

'She's fine. Auntie Nora looks after her when I'm working, and Holly adores her. Uncle Billy's a bit difficult though.' I bit my lip.

'He'll come round,' said Leo, squeezing my arm.

Leo gave me a lift to Auntie Nora's in the white van that Savage Sweets had supplied to him.

'Have you seen Ciaran at all?' I asked.

'Yes, I saw him the other day with your Mam.'

'How is he? How's Mam?' I asked, a catch in my voice.

'They seem fine. Your Mam's working from home now.'

'I suppose she has to, now that I'm not there to mind Ciaran,' I said, wishing with all my heart that I was at home, and thinking what a shame it was that I couldn't send them my love.

Leo noticed my sadness and changed the subject. 'Hey, how would you and Holly like to come for a drive on your day off?' he asked.

'That'd be lovely, if you're sure it would all right to take us in your van.'

' 'Course it would,' Leo assured me.

The following Sunday, Leo arrived in the afternoon. He put Holly's pram in the back of the van and drove us to Powerscourt waterfall, where we saw and heard the thunderous roar of the cascading torrents in contrast to the utter silence all around. In a field a short distance away, we had our picnic of lemonade, biscuits and sweets that Leo had brought.

While Holly napped, I told Leo about the real horrors of the Magdalene Laundry and all the awful events that led up to my leaving it. Shocked, he said sadly. 'If you'd only told me all this when I came to see you, I'd have got you out of there somehow.'

I shook my head. 'There was nothing you could have done. The nuns would never have let me keep Holly and I wouldn't have left without her,' I assured him.

'You did the right thing.' Glancing towards the pram Leo said, 'Charles is foolish, he doesn't know what he's missing.'

'Any news of him?' I asked.

'He's OK. He has a flat in the city centre.'

'Has he got someone else?' I held my breath.

'Not that I know of.' A glimmer of excited hope fluttered in me, until Leo continued seriously, 'Listen, Stella, don't pin your hopes on Charles. I'd hate to see you get hurt again . . .'

I knew he was right. I would have to get on with my own life and not waste my time chasing dreams. That didn't mean it didn't still hurt when I thought of Charles Thornton.

'Don't worry, I'm not going to let that happen,' I tried to assure Leo. But even as I said the words, I knew I didn't sound convincing.

Back in Bray, Leo tore a page from a Savage Sweet order form and scribbled the phone number of his flat on it. 'If you want to get away from the house at any time, or just go somewhere, give me a ring.'

'Thanks, Leo,' I said gratefully, folding the page and putting it in my purse.

Auntie Nora insisted that Leo stay for tea. 'He's a nice lad,' she said, when he'd gone home. 'He's a kind-hearted, responsible young man, and good-looking too.'

'He's a good friend,' I agreed. 'And the only contact I have with home.'

'Well, he likes *you* a lot.' She cast a glance at me. 'Do you like him?'

'Yes, I do, but . . . he doesn't make my heart race the way Charles did,' I said sadly.

'He probably knows that he could never live up to the glory of Charles,' Auntie Nora said stiffly.

'I suppose so.'

I looked away.

'Don't set too much store by those romantic notions of yours, Stella. Charles let you down badly.'

'Maybe if I'd got rid of the baby like he suggested, we might be still together.'

'And you wouldn't have Holly,' Auntie Nora pointed out.

'I know, and I couldn't imagine my life without her.' I couldn't imagine life without Charles either, but I couldn't say that to her.

'Promise me you'll forget about him.'

I shook my head. 'I'm sorry Auntie Nora, I can't do that.'

Her smile faded and her eyes had a look of such intense sadness that I could hardly bear to look at them. She leaned forward and took my hand. 'Don't make the same mistake twice, Stella. You'd never forgive yourself and you'd never stop paying for it.' Her voice cracked as she said, 'I love you and Holly. I want the best for you.'

Tears filled my eyes. I blinked them away. Suddenly I felt trapped. I needed to get out. 'I think I'll go for a quick walk to clear my head.' I grabbed my coat and went out.

The evening air was cold and welcome. I walked fast, wondering why I could not make that promise to Auntie

Nora. Was I going to try and catch up with Charles again, or was I going to keep running away for ever? I wasn't sure, but one thing I was certain about was that I was lonely, and I was scared of bringing up Holly all by myself.

Nineteen

One evening in the café, Theresa said to me, 'There's someone looking for you.'

I felt my stomach tighten into a knot, thinking, the nuns! How did they find me?

I heard the sound of a cough and a familiar voice said, 'Hello Stella.'

I turned. And I stood face to face with Charles. Pulling myself together with tremendous effort, taking a deep breath, I said, 'Hello Charles.'

He stepped forward, handsome and sure of himself in a blue shirt and black leather jacket.

'How are you?' he asked, his eyes brighter than ever in his tanned, familiar face.

'Fine, thanks.' Trembling slightly, I tried hard to stop myself from reaching out to touch him.

'When do you finish work?' he asked.

I looked up at the wall clock. 'I've another ten minutes to go.'

'Want me to wait outside for you?'

'If you like.' I tried to sound casual.

He took his crash helmet off the counter and put it under his arm, leaving me staring after him as he walked out.

'Another friend from home?' Theresa asked with a sarcastic grin.

'Yes,' I said, as off-hand as I could manage.

'He's very dishy,' she said. 'You'll have to introduce me.'

I cleared the remaining tables as quickly as I could and wiped them down, barely able to contain the nervous excitement I felt at seeing him again. I grabbed my bag, ran into the toilet, yanking off my apron as I went, sure he'd be gone when I got out. I changed out of my black dress into my jeans and top, combed my hair and put on more lipstick, my insides churning.

Outside, the street was empty. I looked up and down but there was no sign of Charles or his motorbike. He'd probably got fed up waiting and had gone.

'Stella!' I turned to see him walking towards me.

'I thought you'd gone,' I said, trying to hide my relief.

He laughed. 'No, my bike's parked round the corner. Come on. I'll give you a lift home.' He handed me a spare helmet. I put it on and climbed on to the back of his motorbike. We took off and the wind smacked my face and made my eyes smart. I hung on to him as he ripped down to the coast road – and for a moment it was like it used to be. As though we were an ordinary couple on an early-evening jaunt.

Charles braked at the Esplanade and switched off the engine. I tottered as I slid off the bike. He caught me. 'OK?' he asked. The shock of his hands on me made me flinch.

'OK?' he asked again, noticing.

'Yes, fine.' I watched the tensing of his muscles as he parked the bike.

'So, how are you?' he asked, looking deep into my eyes.

'I'm getting on well.' I couldn't look at him for fear of bursting into tears. Being with him was like being in a play, playing a part that I'd rehearsed over and over again and that I still wasn't getting right.

'I heard that you're in Bolton Street,' I said, to fill the following silence.

He nodded. 'Dad can be very persuasive. I didn't have a choice.'

'How was Boston?'

'Fantastic. It's a very exciting place; there is so much to do there. You wouldn't believe the amount of Irish pubs and clubs there are, and everyone's so friendly.'

'You weren't homesick then.'

He looked down at me and laughed. 'You must be joking.'

I winced, but continued making smalltalk. 'Was the work hard?'

'Very. Look, I've got the welts to prove it,' he said, proudly holding out his hands, showing off the rough skin and his broken fingernails. 'I learned a few things from the experience.'

'Oh?'

'How to survive, and how to be one of the lads, and I mean real, grown-up men. They were a great bunch.' Looking closely at me he said, 'It's a big, bad world out there, Stella. You have to do battle every day just to survive.'

'Don't I know it,' I said sarcastically.

He didn't seem to notice. 'It was a great experience,' he went on. 'I wouldn't have missed it for the world. I made such good friends out there that I didn't want to come home.'

As we walked along I listened to his tales of long working days and late night pub-crawls, too dispirited to interrupt. The effort of trying to make polite conversation with him too much for me.

Finally, he turned to me. 'Stella, I've been going on and on, boring you to death. What about you, I heard from Leo that you didn't fare so well?'

'I didn't expect to.' I felt uncomfortable as I said, 'Mam packed me off as fast as she could. As far as she was concerned I'd done the worst thing a daughter could do to a mother.'

Charles said, 'I'm sorry I didn't keep in touch, Stella. I was worried about you, I really was. I wanted to write to you but I didn't know what to say.' I felt myself blush, and looked away. I couldn't bring myself to rake over that time again. 'You got out of there, that's the main thing.'

'Yes, and I'll get a proper job, where there's some sort of training and promotion. Who knows, I might even get the chance to go to college some day.'

'And the baby?' he asked, his eyes hesitant.

'Holly is her name. She's beautiful,' I said, choosing my words carefully.

'Leo told me.'

Taking courage from his smile, I added shyly, 'She's got your eyes.' Thinking of her sent a shiver of happiness down my spine.

'It's getting late, I'd better get you back to her.' He said, then hesitated before asking, 'Could I see her? I mean, if it's all right with you?'

I swallowed. I could say no to him, I thought, but did I have the right to deprive Holly of her father – probably for always if I refused him now.

'She'll be asleep.'

'Just a peek, I won't wake her up.'

Outside Auntie Nora's, Charles switched off the bike engine and then followed me into the house. For a moment we stood in the hall in awkward silence. It didn't feel right that he should follow me up to my bedroom. Auntie Nora and Uncle Billy were in the living room, and I didn't want to wake Holly up so I quietly led the way upstairs, already regretting my decision.

Charles followed me into the bedroom and leaned

over the cot. As he looked down at Holly he gave a start, the way Auntie Nora had done when she first saw her. There was a sadness that he didn't seem to be able to hide. He turned to me. 'She really is beautiful,' he whispered, awe-struck.

At the sound of his voice Holly woke up and whimpered. I lifted her up. 'This is your daddy, sleepyhead,' I told her. 'He's come to see you.'

'Hello, Holly,' Charles whispered.

Holly's lower lip quivered. She pressed her head against me.

'I'll get her a bottle,' I said, and left him upstairs while I went with Holly down to heat her feed. Back upstairs Charles looked on as I fed her. 'Would you like to hold her?' I asked him when the bottle was empty. I held her out to him. 'She won't bite.' I smiled encouragingly at him.

Gingerly, he took her in his arms. As she gazed up at him we exchanged a smile of amusement, and when I went to take her from him he ignored my outstretched arms and kept holding her. 'Holly is a pretty name, it suits you,' he said to her. Turning to me he said, 'I'm sorry I let you down, Stella. I really do regret that.'

I swallowed the hurt feelings coming up. Words hurt like hell, but the look of sadness and loss on his face was worse. 'I'm sure you were lonely,' he said.

'Yes, I was.' I closed my eyes, determined not to let him see how lonely I still was.

'So was I,' he said. Startled, I looked at him. 'I still am,' he said and waited for me to say something. When I didn't say anything, he asked, 'Is that so hard to believe?'

'Well . . . yes, it is.' I took Holly from him and looked away, not wanting to meet his gaze.

He gave me an uncertain smile. 'You don't like me very much, do you?' When I didn't answer he put a hand on my arm. 'I'd better go.' He stood up, kissed Holly on the forehead, 'I think she's adorable, I'd like to see her again sometime if that's OK, Stella.' He looked as if he meant it.

I met his gaze and nodded, not trusting myself to speak. I saw him to the door and stood in awkward silence as I waited for him to go.

He leaned towards me, kissed me on the cheek. The nearness of him was too much. I stepped back, desperate for him to go.

'Thank you for letting me see Holly. I'll keep in touch this time, I promise,' he said.

I opened the front door and he stepped out. I shut the door after him as quickly and quietly as I could.

Once back in the bedroom, the floodgates opened and all the emotion that I'd kept the lid tightly shut on rushed out. Tears fell on Holly's brow as I rocked her to sleep, going over the whole evening: the way Charles had looked at me; the excitement in his eyes when he talked about Boston and his new-found pals. But most of all, the way his eyes had lit up when he'd taken Holly in his arms.

I had to admit to myself that I still wanted him. I wanted him with every fibre of my being, more than I'd ever wanted anything in my life. His visit had only served to reinforce all the things about him that I'd missed – not just the birth of Holly, but the years of her life to come. I wanted everything to be like it had been before. Then I remembered that this was the same boy who had abandoned me to the wolves for his own selfish reasons.

I didn't tell Auntie Nora about his visit. She would have been disapproving and I certainly didn't need a lecture.

'Did you enjoy yourself last night?' Theresa asked, the next day in the café.

Blushing, I avoided her eyes. 'He's gorgeous. Who is he?' she persisted. I fled to serve the tables at the first opportunity, glad of the customers, and the din.

During my break, Theresa said, 'You can tell me all about him, I'm good at keeping secrets.'

'There's nothing to tell.'

'Looks like a heartbreaker,' she teased.

'Maybe,' I said, thinking that at least he'd come looking for me. In time he might get to know Holly and be a proper father to her.

As the day went on I grew calmer, savouring all the best bits of our meeting. Theresa looked at me. 'Is that a secret little smile I see?' she asked.

* * *

Leo came to see me a few days later. 'I heard that Charles came to see you,' he said.

'Yes, he did.' I said. 'It was very awkward, especially when he asked to see Holly.' After a pause I went on, 'He said he'd keep in touch, but I'm not so sure.'

'Do you want him to?'

'Yes.'

'You still hold a torch for him?'

'I was hoping I wouldn't. I thought I'd be able to talk about what had happened to me, but I couldn't. Did he say anything to you?'

'He said that he was very taken with Holly. He didn't mention you.'

I looked away, the tears starting.

Leo frowned. 'I'm sorry, I seem to do nothing but upset you,' he said miserably.

'No, not at all.' I forced myself to smile. 'It's just that I was coping well, or I thought I was, until I saw him. Then it all came flooding back,' I said hopelessly.

'Cheer up, you're the one who got the best deal. You've got Holly.'

'And he's probably got another girl, anyway.' I could feel jealousy stirring inside me at the thought of Charles with another girl. I imagined him lounging in a bar with someone beautiful, sophisticated, nothing like me.

Leo's kind, sympathetic eyes were on me. 'He hasn't mentioned anyone to me'.

'Then he wouldn't, knowing that you and I are in touch.'

Leo looked at me speculatively. 'I don't really know,' he said. And his expression was suddenly sad. 'I'd better be OK,' he said quickly, leaving me looking after him, wondering what I'd said.

Twenty

On my next afternoon off, I took Holly for a walk. I pulled up the hood of her pram against the wind, went down the hill, under the bridge, and crossed the road to the promenade. I breathed in the salt air and watched the waves as I walked along, reminded of Knocknacree and blissful, innocent days spent gathering shells on the beach with Ciaran. At the harbour I sat on the wall and watched a boy skimming stones; one stone bounced over the surface, ripples spread outwards, then all calm again until he took up another stone. I watched the waves merging then falling away, thinking of the evenings I'd spent on the beach with Charles; his warm body protecting me from the cold wind. Shivering at the memory, I stood up to make my way back. At the corner of our road I saw a boy standing with his eyes fixed on me. As I walked past him other boys appeared from behind the wall. They too stared at me. I kept walking.

'Hello!' one of them called after me.

I turned round. The first boy came striding up to me, blocked my way. 'Haven't see you before. Not from round here, are you?' When I didn't answer he looked into the pram. 'This your brat?' he asked.

'Mind your own business,' I said, angrily. But my anger was quickly replaced by fear when they surrounded the pram.

'Excuse me.' I tried to walk past.

The first boy stepped in front of me. 'What's your name?' he asked. I kept my eyes downcast. He stood looking at me, calmly. 'I said what's your name?' he repeated with a strange smile on his face, as if this was a game of some sort.

'I'm not telling you,' I said, looking past him, trying to keep calm

One of the other boys said, 'Come on, tell us, we're only trying to be friendly,' giving the pram a shove. Playfully, the first boy grabbed the pram and jerked it from side to side. The pink teddy bear fell out. Holly woke up and began to cry.

'Stop it!' I shouted, grabbing his arm.

He burst out laughing. 'Try and stop me.'

From nowhere a cop appeared. 'What's going on here?' he asked, flicking suspicious eyes from one of us to the other.

The first boy scrabbled to his feet. 'Nothing, Officer,' he said.

'You all right?' he asked me.

'Yes,' I said shakily.

Turning to the boys he said angrily, 'Clear off and leave

this poor girl alone.' Go on; get off home before you get into more trouble.'

They sloped off, heads down, the cop watching them until they were out of sight.

'This your baby?' He lifted the cover of the pram, looked under the blankets.

'No, she's my aunt's,' I said, convinced he'd know I was lying.

'You live round here?'

'No, I'm here on holidays.'

A woman I recognised as one of Auntie Nora's nosy neighbours stopped on her way by. 'I know this girl, Officer. She's the niece of my neighbour, Nora. Nora's taken her in because she can't go home on account of having the baby out of wedlock,' she said.

I clutched the pram as the Garda scrutinised me. 'Keep away from the likes of those boys. I know them and I can tell you they're up to no good,' he warned.

'Yes, Officer,' I said, shaking.

He got on his bike and cycled off.

I went back to Auntie Nora's as fast as I could, taking the short cut through the gap in the woods and going in the back gate. As soon as I got into the house I burst into tears, then Holly began to cry. There was no one in. I lifted Holly out of her pram and held her tightly as I got her bottle out of the fridge. She felt firm and strong in my arms. 'It's so scary,' I said to her, the tears coursing down my cheeks as I heated the

211

bottle. 'I don't know what to do.' I fed her and her tiny hand clutched the bottle. Her eyes held mine, dark and trusting. Holding her was comforting. I didn't feel so alone.

After I'd put Holly down, I washed our clothes to stop myself thinking about what had happened. With each swoosh of water the present faded and the Magdalene Laundry reclaimed me, as well as the desperate loneliness I'd felt there. I realised that the real world was just as hostile as the convent and the nuns had been.

Auntie Nora came in from shopping, Uncle Billy on her heels.

'Nora, Kavanagh's shop has been robbed again,' he told her.

'No!' Auntie said aghast. 'Did they take much?'

'Two days' takings. Sheila didn't have time to go to the bank yesterday.'

My aunt shook her head, 'That's shocking.'

'The guards know who they are. Youngsters from the other end.'

'Well, I hope they catch them.'

'They will, and God help them when they do.' Looking at me he said pointedly, 'Gone to the dogs, the kids of today. No decency in them at all.'

After tea, I put Holly to bed and stayed in my room and began a long letter to Maeve. Then I fell into bed, exhausted – the day's events still swirling vaguely in my head.

An electrifying ring on the doorbell woke me with a start next morning.

'Stella!' Auntie Nora called up the stairs.

'Just a minute,' I called back, getting out of bed, tidying my hair. I went downstairs in my dressing gown, astonished to find the Garda from the previous day standing there, another thin-lipped Garda beside him.

'Garda Kelly wants a word with you, Stella,' a perplexed Auntie Nora said.

'Yes?' I asked, in a shaky voice.

'Hello, Stella. We'd like to ask you a few questions,' the first Garda said.

'Like your previous address?' the thin-lipped cop asked.

I gave him my home address, and as he wrote it down in his notebook I prayed that this visit might be about the boys on the corner, and Kavanagh's shop, and nothing to do with me.'

The thin-lipped cop's next words shattered that sliver of hope. 'According to our records you escaped from the Magdalene Laundry, in Donnybrook, on the twentieth of February.' He raised his eyes and looked tersely into my face.

His words fell like bullets on my ears. My legs turned to jelly as I nodded my head.

'Go and get dressed. We're taking you back there.' Everything went quiet. I stopped breathing for a second.

'Hold on a minute, Sergeant Dillon,' Auntie Nora said. 'Stella is my niece. I took her out of the laundry.'

'There is no record of that, Mrs Doran. We're here to take her and the baby back.' Thin Lips's steely eyes were on me.

'No, I'm not going,' I burst out.

He gave me a long, hard look. 'I'm afraid you have no choice.'

'We've given her a home here,' Auntie Nora protested. 'Stella and her baby are properly looked after.'

'Mrs Doran, you're breaking the law by harbouring them.' Turning to me he said, 'Get dressed and get your baby dressed, we have orders to take you back. You have ten minutes to be out of here.'

'I'm not going back to that awful place.' I sat down in shock at the kitchen table.

'I'm sorry,' he said, unrepentant. 'But the Sisters have registered you as missing. You have to go back to the convent.'

The first Garda said, more gently, 'I know you're a decent, law-abiding citizen, Mrs Doran, but if it gets found out that I knew she was here and hadn't reported it, I'd be in serious trouble.'

Uncle Billy came in. He'd been out for some milk. His eyes widened at the sight of the officers. After Thin Lips had filled him in, Uncle Billy held his palms up. 'I didn't know anything about this, Sergeant, honest I didn't.' It was pathetic. Auntie Nora glared at him but he ignored her. 'Go upstairs and pack your bags at once,' he told me. 'You need to face up to what you've done, Stella.'

Thin Lips's face softened. 'I'm glad somebody's got the right attitude, Mr Doran.'

Pushing past Uncle Billy, Auntie Nora took hold of my hands and squeezed them tight. 'Come on, I'll help you pack,' she said, shutting the door on the cops, leaving Uncle Billy chatting to them.

As my aunt bustled around the spare room, putting things in a case, I stood numbly over Holly's carrycot. She looked so small and vulnerable as she lay there, squashed up in sleep. 'Its all wrong, she's *my* baby,' I said to Auntie Nora.

'She is, and I'm not letting this happen, Stella, love. I've got an idea. I'll keep them talking while you sneak out the back. Ring Leo from the phone box on the corner. Have you got his phone number?'

I got out my purse, hunted for the Savage Sweets order form. 'Here it is.'

'Right. Get dressed quickly while I put a few things in a bag for you.'

My legs like jelly, I sneaked Holly downstairs and out of the back door. I turned to say goodbye to Auntie Nora. 'Go, hurry,' she hissed, handing me a small case. 'You must go to Leo, he'll help you.' Her voice was urgent. 'I'll get in touch with you later on,' she whispered, holding me to her and then kissing Holly, before going back to distract the guards.

I crept up the garden and through the gate in the hedge. I was out, running like mad up the road to the phone box on the corner. I took out my purse, got out three pennies, put them in the slot, and dialled Leo's number. I kept my eyes on the road while it rang. When a woman answered, I pressed button A.

'Is Leo there, please?'

'Who's speaking?'

'Stella.'

'Hold on a moment, I'll go and see.'

There was the bang of the phone and the hollow sound of footsteps. I looked through the phone box window, marking the distance I was from the trees in case I had to make a run for it again. Panic-stricken, I was about to put the phone down, when Leo's voice said, 'Stella?'

'Leo! The cops have come to take me back to the laundry.'

'No!'

'I've managed to give them the slip. I'm the phone box at the end of Auntie Nora's road, just before the entrance to the woods. There's a big gate, a notice, and a path.'

'I know it.'

'Will you come and get me?' I said, in a panic-stricken rush.

'Go into the woods and hide. I'll come and find you.'

'Hurry, Leo.'

'I'll be there as soon as I can.'

I replaced the receiver and left the phone box, walking as fast as I could towards the woods, glancing over my shoulder at the road as I went. When I heard the sound of a car, I went further into the woods and waited, crouched behind a big tree, telling Holly that she mustn't cry. Blissfully unaware of the drama surrounding us, she gurgled and smiled. I stayed still, barely breathing, as footsteps approached. A twig snapped close by. I nearly jumped out of my skin as Garda Kelly's voice, thick with frustration, said, 'Right or left?' With growing terror I watched them stomp past me up the hill, Garda Kelly with his head tilted, listening, Thin Lips with his head down, like a tracker dog. Cradling Holly in my arms, I dreaded their return. But they carried on, their heads turning right and left. I stayed still, scared to move a muscle until I heard the engine of a car starting up. They were gone, but they'd be back. I had to get out of the woods fast.

Holly began to cry. I rocked her, telling her that Leo would come soon, and begging her to hold on a bit longer. 'You're all I have, I'm not going to let them take you away from me,' I said, pressing her to me.

A shrill whistle pierced the air. It was Leo. I got to my feet and tried to whistle back, but I couldn't – my mouth had dried up. Footsteps approached. I peered out from behind the tree to see Leo walking towards me.

'Are you all right?' he whispered as he drew close.

'I've never been so scared in all my life.' He put his arm round my shoulders. My whole body collapsed into his.

'Come on, while the coast is clear,' he said gently.

'What if they come back?'

'We'll be long gone.'

He took Holly from me and led the way down the path. I followed him in silence. His van was hidden in the lay-by near the gate. I took Holly and got in. Leo started the engine. 'We'd better get out of here fast, before someone sees us,' he said.

My heart was in my mouth as we drove off. I glanced at Leo. He looked scared too. He stopped outside a tall, terraced house, took a drowsy Holly from me, and carried her up the steps, through the hall and up a flight of stairs and into a dingy room, me following.

Holly woke up and started howling. I got her bottle out of the carrier bag.

'I'll get us something to eat while you feed her?' Leo said, and went into the kitchenette.

I sat on the couch and gave Holly her bottle, looking at the threadbare carpet with bald patches here and there, and the old, dark furniture. But it was refuge, and soon the delicious smell of grilling bacon and toast wafted out and I realised I was starving. Leo set the table and brought out the food.

'So, what do I do now?' I asked.

'You can stay here as long as you like. I can protect you,' he said firmly.

'It's far too much to ask of you, Leo.'

Leo didn't look at me. 'It would be a safer option.'

'What about your flatmate, won't he mind?'

Leo shook his head. 'Not for a while. Liam's away on holiday. Honestly, Stella, it's fine. I want to look after you and Holly.'

'It might get you into a lot of trouble . . .'

He shrugged. 'Let me worry about that.'

'Thanks, Leo, it's very kind of you.' I cleared my throat in an effort not to cry as we regarded one another.

'Do you want me to let Charles know that you're here?' he asked.

I thought about it for a moment. 'Yes, I think he should know.'

'I'll give him a shout and I'll call into your Auntie Nora's to let her know that you're safe, she'll be anxious about you.'

'Thanks Leo.'

When Leo went out I put Holly down to sleep in yet another drawer, then sat by the window, watching and waiting for his return, my stomach in a knot at the thought of seeing Charles again.

That evening, when I heard Leo's footsteps on the stairs, I rushed to open the door.

'Did you see him?' I asked.

'He wasn't there. I left a message for him to phone me. Don't worry, everything will be all right. I promise.'

I wished I could believe him.

Twenty-One

That night, I lay in Liam's narrow bed while Leo slept on the sofa, wondering what I should do next. Holly was on the floor beside me in a drawer. Next morning when Leo had gone to work, I tidied up the flat for something to do while I waited for Leo to return.

In the afternoon, Auntie Nora came to see me. She brought some of our clothes and a big bag of groceries.

'I was so relieved when Leo called to see me; it's so kind of him to let you stay,' she said.

'He says he doesn't mind.'

'Sergeant Dillon's been round, asking if I've heard from you. I told him that I havn't. I could see by him that he didn't believe me. I'm sure he's keeping an eye on the place — and me — so I'd better not stay long.' She paused. 'You'll have to get away, Stella, if you want to give them the slip for good.'

'Where to?'

'To London, to your dad; they can't come after you there.'

'London!'

'Yes, and soon. I'll write to your dad this evening to let him know to expect you, and I'll buy your ticket for the mail boat.'

'You have his address?'

'Yes, he wrote to us a while back.'

'I'm sorry I've caused you so much trouble,' I said regretfully, but she wouldn't hear of it.

'It'll be worth it all if you can get to keep this little mite,' she said, giving Holly a goodbye kiss on the cheek.

When Leo returned, I told him about Auntie Nora's visit and her plans for me to go and stay with Dad.

'It's probably for the best,' he agreed, reluctantly, I could tell.

'Did you hear from Charles?'

'Not yet, but I'm sure he'll get in touch.' Leo sounded confident, but his eyes were doubtful.

Auntie Nora returned the next day with a ticket to Holyhead and a crisp ten-pound note for the journey. 'I've written to your dad to tell him the time of your arrival. He'll be at Euston station to meet you.'

I hugged her gratefully. Suddenly, I wasn't scared any more. I knew that Dad wouldn't abandon me. He would love Holly and would want to protect us.

Leo phoned Charles again, and found him in. He told him what had happened and that I was planning on going to live in England. Charles said that he would come and see me that evening. As soon as Holly was asleep I had a bath, changed and put on my make-up, wanting to look good for him. When I heard the knock on the door I answered it immediately, and came face to face with an unsmiling Charles.

'You're going away?' he asked, barging in the room.

'I have to, before they find me and take me back to the convent.'

Charles looked at me coldly. 'Don't *I* have a say in the matter?'

I looked up at him in surprise. 'I'm not going on a whim, Charles. The cops are after me. They'll take me back to the convent. They'll take Holly from me if I stay here.'

'And you think that it won't make any difference to me if you take Holly away.'

I could feel myself going red in the face as I said, 'You didn't seem to care much before.'

He folded his arms in a defensive gesture. 'It's different now that I've seen her. I was looking forward to getting to know her.'

'So you expect me to stay and risk losing her.' I glared at him, rage rising in me.

'You wouldn't lose her. I'd make sure of that. My parents would sort out the legalities.'

'You mean they'd take her over.'

'No, that's not what I'm saying.'

I took a deep breath, forced myself to meet his gaze. 'You dumped me once before, left me to rot in the Magdalene Laundry, and now you want me to hand over my daughter to you and your parents. Well, I'm sorry, I can't do that. Maybe you've forgotten what happened this last year, but I haven't.'

'You weren't the only one who was upset. I was too,' he said sheepishly.

'You could have fooled me.'

He crossed the room to stand beside me. 'Holly's my daughter. I care about her.'

'You kept that fact well-hidden until now. All along you knew what I was going through and you never once got in touch. You left me all on my own to get on with it.'

'I know I did and I'm sorry, Stella.'

'Sorry!' My blood boiled 'You ran away and now you think that by saying "sorry" you can put everything right.'

He flinched. 'I ran away because I didn't have a choice. My parents went crazy when they heard that I'd got you pregnant. My dad threatened me with all sorts if I saw you again. I couldn't handle it. I felt awful about it. I kept wondering about you. I missed you.'

'You could have written to me.'

'And what could I have said? I didn't have anything to offer you at the time, and I wasn't sure how you'd be with me – how you'd feel towards me. Then, seeing

Holly made me realise what I was missing.' He looked at me pleadingly. 'I'm scared at the thought of losing her again. You've got to believe me, I'm telling you the truth.'

I took a deep breath to control myself. 'I'm scared of losing her too, that's why I'm going to England, where it's safe for us both.'

'Don't go, Stella,' he pleaded. 'Stay. I'll get a job. You and Holly can come and live with me.' I breathed in his smell as he moved closer to me. 'I want to be with Holly, and you.'

I should have been thrilled to hear those words, but I wasn't. 'Until you run off again.' I knew I was being harsh but I had to say what I felt.

'You really think I'd do that?' he said, a painful expression on his face.

'You did it once before.'

'It's different now.'

'No it isn't. You're starting college in September. Your dad'll go crazy if you mess that up again.'

He looked at me angrily. 'I suppose this is on your Auntie Nora's advice. This is all her doing, isn't it? She wants to get you away from me, doesn't she?'

'This is my decision. It's got nothing to do with Auntie Nora.' I looked up at him. 'I have to get away from you.'

'Why?'

I looked at him levelly. 'We both know it's over between us, but it still hurts every time I see you. All the old feelings are there.' I felt empty inside, so desperate for what we had that we couldn't get back. Suddenly, my resolve not to break down deserted me. The floodgates opened.

Charles caught me, held me against his broad shoulders while I wept. 'Don't cry,' he said lamely.

'I can't help it,' I croaked.

In the awful silence that followed, the heartbreak of parting once more came crashing in on me. The old wounds opened up, and with them all the old emotions. I had to do something before I drowned in them.

'Please go, Charles,' I said, moving away from him.

He looked at me, then finally shook his head. 'If that's what you want.'

'Yes. It's what I want,' I said briskly.

At that, he walked out of the room without looking back.

As the front door slammed shut, I felt a terrible emptiness inside. For the rest of the evening I thought of everything Charles had said, and began to wonder whether the love I'd felt for him, he'd really felt for me, too.

Leo returned to find me in tears. I told him what had happened. 'I hate to see you upset, Stella,' he said. I saw the genuine concern in his face and hoped that being involved in the mess that was my life wouldn't hurt him.

'I'll get over it, I did before.'

'I suppose so,' he said doubtfully.

The next day I packed Holly's bottles in a hold-all Leo lent me at the last minute. When Leo came in from work I was ready to go. I was anxious to start my new life.

Twenty-Two

Disguised in some old-fashioned clothes Leo had cadged from his landlady, and wearing her high heels, scarf and pancake stick, we drove to the mail boat. We chatted all the way, careful to avoid any mention of Charles.

At Dun Laoghaire harbour I joined the queue of people waiting to embark. Leo carried Holly as far as the checkpoint. Passing a police officer, we looked like a married couple.

'I'd better take her from here,' I said, getting my ticket out of my bag.

Will you be all right on your own?' he asked, anxiously surveying the crowd surging forward.

'Yes, Dad'll be waiting at Euston station. Thanks, Leo, for everything. You've been a true friend.' I gave him a sisterly kiss on the cheek.

'I wish you didn't have to go,' he said sadly, brushing my cheek with his lips, like he did that day he came to see me in the laundry. 'Take care of yourself, and Holly.' His eyes were full of sadness as he said, 'I'll always be here for you if you want me.'

I sagged against him; the bursts of goodbyes exploding round me like a bad dream. He gave me a bear hug. 'Give me a ring as soon as you get there.' I nodded, too charged up to speak. With a final wave he was gone.

I put Holly into her pram and pushed it through the double doors, walking down a long, draughty corridor and up the gangplank. As I stepped on to the boat I hesitated, but the loud hoot of the horn and the surging crowd pushed me forward. Up on deck, Holly in my arms, I caught sight of Leo waving to me amid all the other waving people. I waved back, smiling through my tears.

As the boat slipped out slowly between the harbour piers, Dun Laoghaire shrank back into the pale lilac sky. Seagulls wheeled overhead, their mournful cries a lament to my leaving. To the left the lights of Dublin twinkled in the mist, giving the ugly city an innocent, fairytale look. A cold wind blew up as the boat turned right for Holyhead.

Out in the bay, great waves rushed towards the prow of the boat. I stared at the grey, immense sea that stretched all the way to the horizon, the fairy lights receding into the distant, misty sky. Holding Holly tight, told her that we would cope. We had to. Then I took her below deck to a corner of the warm lounge and fed her. She slept for the rest of the journey.

At Holyhead we boarded the train for Crew, from where we had to change for Euston station. We both slept most of the way there.

Dad was outside the ticket barrier, waving and smiling.

'Dad!' I cried out, hardly believing my eyes, almost running with my pram, breathless with excitement at seeing him again.

'Stella! It's great to see you,' he said, smiling broadly, his eyes shining with tears as he came to meet me.

He looked different. He was spruced up in a buff-coloured jacket, brown slacks, white shirt and a brightly patterned tie. His neatly trimmed hair made his jaw look longer, and there was a soft fold in his neck that hadn't been there before.

He hugged me. 'Nora told me everything. I was outraged at what happened to you. If only I'd known – I'd have come straight home and taken you out of that barbaric place,' he said, shaking his head.

'Well, I'm here now, Dad, and this is Holly.'

He stooped over the pram, a gleam of anticipation in his eyes as he looked into it. I held my breath as he looked at her for a long time. A shy smile spread over his face as he said, 'So you're Holly, and to think that I've only just heard about you.' She smiled up at him. 'She's the livin' image of you,' he said with awe and wonder. 'Come on, let's get you back to my place.'

We left the station, Dad pushing the pram purposefully, his back straight, pride in his broad shoulders, me following. Outside, he hailed a cab. I took Holly out of her pram while he folded it up. We were driven through streets of screeching cars and red buses to Dad's flat. It was in a plain grey house in a row of drab houses in Westbourne Grove. There were letters on an old hallstand in the dark hallway. Electric meters lined the wall.

Dad opened the door to his flat and switched on the light. The living-room wallpaper was old and stained. There was a Formica-topped table and chairs at one end, a couch and two chairs at the other. Books lay scattered on a small table with a lamp on it. There was emptiness about it, as if nobody lived in it at all. Dad put his hand on my arm and tilted his head towards Holly. 'Bathroom's down the hall, bedroom next to it. You can see to Holly while I get the dinner started – roast chicken do you?'

'Delicious,' I said, realising at that moment that I was.

'Great!' Grinning like a Cheshire cat, he got to work in the tiny kitchen.

I changed Holly and fed her while Dad cooked. Over dinner I told him the whole story. Detailing all the events that led up to Holly's birth, I left nothing out.

'But why on earth didn't your Mam tell me about it?' he sighed, perplexed.

'She thought it would worry you too much.'

'I would have come home, and I wouldn't have consulted Father Cooney either. The man's a fool. He had no right to send you away, and neither had your mother without consulting me first.' With tears in his eyes he said, 'I would have never have permitted it. I'd have taken care of you myself.'

I bowed my head. 'Don't be hard on Mam. She didn't

know what else to do. She didn't want you to lose your job over me.'

'All the same she should have told me.' Leaning towards me he said, 'I'm sorry you had to go through so much, Stella, there was no need for it.'

'It was my own fault. I made a fool of myself with Charles. I'm sorry, Dad,' I said tearfully.

'I'm sorry that I wasn't there when you needed me, Stella, but you have your lovely baby now and there's no time for regrets.' He covered my hand with his big strong one. 'You'll find your feet,' he said. 'And I'll help you.'

'Thanks, Dad.'

That night I slept in his hard, narrow bed while he slept on the couch, Holly in her pram beside me. Holly's cries woke me up the next morning. For a second I didn't know where I was. I pulled the curtains, looked out at the grimy buildings. Sunlight slanted across the black fireplace, highlighting the dust on the mantlepiece. I got dressed and took Holly into the kitchen.

Dad was making breakfast, padding around in his stockinged-feet so as not to wake us. I stood in the frame of the door and watched him.

'Good morning, my sleepy beauties.' He smiled at Holly. She tilted her head towards him and smiled. 'You'll need a bit of nourishment for a day of sight-seeing.'

'Aren't you going to work?'

'No. I'm taking time off to show my only daughter a bit of culture. London's the best city in the world. There's so much for you to see. So, come on, eat up and we'll get started,' he said, taking plates of scrambled eggs and toast over to the already-set Formica table.

Later, we walked up the empty street named Westbourne Grove to the Underground. We queued up at the ticket office. The rattle of the coins made me vaguely homesick for the ticket office in Knocknacree. Dad bought our tickets and we descended a long escalator to a dark tunnel and a platform, full of advertising posters, to wait for the tube. People gathered silently. When the train came roaring in, Holly burst into tears at the sound of it. Dad lifted her up and folded her into his coat. We stood to one side to let passengers out, then Dad got on with Holly and I followed him into the carriage. The train screeched out of the station. It shuddered and rocked from side to side as it raced through the tunnel. We sat on opposite sides of a window, watching each other's reflections. A voice called out the name of the next station. At each stop people jammed up the doorways in their hurry to get off the train.

At Embankment I followed Dad as he made his way to the escalators with the pram. I stumbled against the metal step but I caught myself in time, then kept my eyes on the metal steps as it climbed steeply upwards. Finally we were out walking along by the river, the cool breeze welcoming after the stifling air of the Underground. The magnificent buildings on either side, golden in the morning light, were reflected in the still water. We went to the Tower of London, where tourists were queuing up.

'Would you like to go in?' Dad asked.

'No thanks.'

'Look at your face,' he laughed. 'You'd swear you were about to lose your own life.'

'This is a lovely place,' I said later as we sat sipping coffee in a Lyons Corner House that overlooked a park.

'I walked everywhere when I first came here, trying to get to know the place,' Dad said. 'I know every inch of it by now.'

'You've really settled down here, Dad,' I said, amazed at his ease in the strange city.

He tilted his head back and smiled. 'Not really. I've never got used to it. I miss the open spaces. I miss home; it's so much part of me. I'd like to go back, take a walk along the shore. Go fishing with Ciaran.'

'He'd love that, he misses you so much.'

He leaned towards me. 'You never know, I might just do that.' A shaft of sunlight caught Dad's eyes. They sparkled, lighting up his face. 'Come on,' he said, draining his cup. 'Let's explore some more.'

We walked to Knightsbridge, peered into gorgeous shop windows, passed posh restaurants, the air heavy with the delicious smell of herbs and spices. The traffic buzzed past. I looked sideways at Dad, pushing the pram, his shoulders shifting from side to side as he walked.

At Park Lane we stopped to admire the tall houses

with their great front doors and windows overlooking the park and trees. 'I couldn't imagine living in a house like that. All that space to myself,' I said to Dad.

'Sure, maybe they're not happy either,' he said.

I thought of our house at the end of our street, Mam in her chair at the window, sewing, and her eyes ever-vigilant.

That evening over supper, Dad grinned wickedly at me. 'Treat this as a little holiday, Stella,' he said. 'When you've seen the sights you're going back home.'

'What?' The shock almost sent me reeling backwards. 'You can't send me back, Mam won't have me there.'

'She will if I'm there with you.'

'You're coming too?'

'Yes. I've decided to take you back home myself. We'll sort this out once and for all.'

I gazed at him, open-mouthed. 'What about your job?'

'I've been doing a lot of overtime. I've a bit of money put by. So that'll keep me going until I get a job. The building trade's on the up back home. Several of the men I worked with have gone back and got good jobs. One fella got a job on a building site in Wicklow town. He'd put in a good word for me. I'd be there to help you take care of Holly. Strikes me that you need your father, and Holly needs her grandfather.' He leaned towards Holly, blew her a kiss.

'Oh, Dad, that would be great.'

He beamed at me. 'I'll have a bit of a holiday first.'

'But what about the neighbours, Dad?'

'What about them? You're not the first girl in Knocknacree to have a baby without being married, and you won't be the last.'

I still had doubts. 'Mam's so dead against me being there.'

'She needs me there to get some sense into her.' He sat back and smiled. 'I might even buy a little car. The roads over there are quiet; it's not like Piccadilly Circus, is it?'

I had a vision of Dad pulling up outside our house on Station Row, hooting the horn, Ciaran running out, his little shoulders raised in surprise.

'Oh, Dad, that would be terrific.'

'I've got the garden to do; I bet it's in a right old state.' He was thoughtful. 'I'd still help out in the Youth Club and I'd take Holly for walks in her pram. Just to look over the fields and woods, see the vast, open sky, would be wonderful. I could get the binoculars out, show Holly the stars. I've missed all that. I've missed out on some of Ciaran's growing up. I'm not going to miss out on Holly's.' He sighed. 'I need to get back to the old life. It's all part of me, it's what I am.'

It was strange to even think of going back to Knocknacree — yet it was what I craved.

Dad walked up the path first. 'Eileen?' he called out, as he opened the door. I stood on the gravel, listening to his heavy footstep across the floorboards of the hallway. I heard him stop, heard the kitchen door opening and the sound of the radio.

'Jim!' Mam's piercing cry wrenched the air.

I listened to their voices, Dad explaining why he had surprised her with a visit, my eyes on the house. There were loose bricks here and there and the paint was peeling on the window frames.

'I've brought someone with me,' I heard Dad say. I moved the pram back into the shadows as far as I could, dreading her coming and finding us, and longing for it at the same time. All during our journey back Dad and I hadn't spoken of this meeting, too fearful of what the outcome might be.

'Who?' The hallway echoed her voice as she came out.

'Stella!' she gasped, her eyes frantically searching my face.

Dad was out beside her in a flash. She stared at me. I kept my eyes on Ciaran's hopscotch squares on the path, afraid to meet her gaze.

'Have you lost your tongue?' Dad said to me.

'Hello, Mam.'

She caught the sleeve of my coat and drew me to her. I could feel her chest heaving as she pressed me to her.

'Come and meet Holly,' Dad said, pointing to the pram.

'Holly?' Suddenly everything that had happened in the last year was condensed into that name as her eyes strained towards the pram. She approached it gingerly, her hands in a tight clasp as she bent over it. 'Ah, no!' she said.

My throat swelled and threatened to burst as I watched her hands slowly reach out and lift Holly up. I could feel the knot of all my grief unravel as she cradled her. Dad put his hand on her shoulder and drew her to him. Holly's white stocked feet dangled between them.

'Isn't she beautiful?' Dad said.

I held my breath.

'Yes, just like Stella,' she said gazing at Holly, tears shining in her eyes.

At that moment Ciaran came tearing up the road. 'Dad! Stella! 'What're you doing here?' he called out at the top of his voice.

Dad went to meet him. 'Hey buddy!' he cried, lifting him up in the air, twirling him around.

'I brought your baby niece home to meet you,' Dad said, putting him down.

'That's Stella's baby?' Ciaran said, staring at Holly, then at me as if seeing me too for the first time. 'Did you bring them here, Dad?'

'Yes, son.'

Before I could get a word in, Ciaran said, 'Are the police going to come and try and take them away?' His voice was thin and reedy.

Dad shook his head. 'Over my dead body,' he said. I felt the tears behind my eyes threatening to spill over. Dad drew Ciaran to him, roughed up his hair. 'Stella and her baby are home for good.'

Mam opened her mouth to say something, but her breath caught in her throat and no words came.

'She's very small,' Ciaran said, staring at Holly.

At that moment the door of Maeve's house burst open. 'Stella!' She rushed forward, her arms stretched wide across the blanket of hedge. 'You're back, I can't believe it. I missed you so much.'

'I missed you too.' We hugged one another.

'Let's see your baby.'

Mam went to the hedge, Holly firmly in the crook of her arm.

'Oh, look, she's so beautiful,' Maeve said, gazing at her in wonder.

Mrs Ruane came to her door and looked out to see what the commotion was.

'Let's go inside first,' Dad said, carrying in the bags.

'I'll be out later,' I promised Maeve.

I took Holly to my bedroom, stopping for a moment in the hallway before turning the handle of the door. I looked around at neat and tidy space: the white quilted bed, the plumped-up pillows, the row of wire hangers in the empty space of the wardrobe, my few treasured books on my shelf. The room seemed to have shrunk. The little white china dish which held the bracelet Charles had given me for my birthday was in my top drawer where I'd left it. I lifted it up to the light, heard the echo of

Charles's laughter trapped in its sparkling chain, felt the touch of his hand as he placed it around my neck, in their smoothness.

I changed Holly and made my way back to the kitchen. Mam was at the stove making tea. My gaze travelled across the kitchen: the dresser with the blue willow-patterned plates, postcards stuck here and there between them; the sewing machine, the Bakelite radio on the shelf above it with its gold mesh dial. Everything was the same, as if nothing in our lives had changed.

Mam caught my eye. 'It's been a long time,' she said. I said nothing. She turned down the heat under a pan. 'I couldn't bear to hear Ciaran cry in the night when you left. I could tell by the way he'd be watching the door while I'd be getting his breakfast ready that he was hoping you'd walk in.' She clasped her neck as if in defence. The kettle screeched. She turned the sausages with a flick of her wrist. 'You've been through alot, Stella,' she said. I felt myself go tense as we regarded one another. 'When I heard that you'd escaped from the convent I wanted to help you, but I didn't know where you'd gone.' I looked at her. She looked sheepish as she said, 'Dad said that you went to Auntie Nora's.'

'Auntie Nora was very kind to me when she came to see me at the laundry. I knew she wouldn't throw me out.'

Mam closed her eyes, hurt and guilty, for a second. 'What about Charles? Did he know that you'd run away?'

'Yes, he didn't want me to go to England.'

'I suppose that's understandable; he is the child's father.'

'If he'd come forward sooner may be . . .' I stopped. 'What's the point of going over it all. He didn't.'

Mam put her hand across mine. I felt the tremble in it as I met her gaze. I saw the sorrow in the sharp ridge of her cheekbones, and the tearful eyes that flickered from Holly back to me again. I longed for her to say that she was glad to see me and that I was welcome home. But I knew it anyway; I'd be content with that.

Holly cried. 'I'll heat her bottle,' I said, glad of the distraction.

After tea, when Holly was finally asleep, Maeve and I sat side by side on the doorstep of her house. Her hair was shining; her skin was smooth and golden. She was taller, all arms and legs. She was growing into a real beauty.

'Tell me everything,' she said, folding her arms across her drawn-up knees. I desperately wanted to tell her all about my life over the past year, but I knew that in giving the details of it I would feel blemished. 'Well, go on, tell me about the convent,' she said, her head tipped towards me encouragingly.

I drew my shoulders together. 'There's not much to tell.'

'There must be something; you ran away, for God's sake.' She took my hand, pressed it encouragingly. 'Where did you go?'

'Auntie Nora's first, but the cops came after me, so I went to London.'

'Were you scared?'

'Yes, but I had no choice.'

'Well, now here you are, home at last, and it's great,' she said comfortingly.

Two boys from further down the street passed by and stared in at us. One nudged one another.

'Did you see Charles?' Maeve asked.

I felt my heart rising in my chest as I thought of him. 'Yes. He wanted to see Holly, and I felt I didn't have the right to stop him. I thought we'd be able to . . . discuss things without all these feelings . . .' I looked away. 'I don't know – the whole thing was too much. In some ways I wish I hadn't seen him at all.'

'You still love him.' It was a statement.

I felt my face flame up as I shook my head. 'It was never the same after I got pregnant.'

'Shame you ever got mixed up with him,' Maeve said, as if she had never considered it before. 'You were different before you started going out with him. And you were so sure of yourself, with your job in the café and everything. I wanted to be like you.'

'Really? I wasn't that sure of myself, I only pretended to be,' I said. While we talked the sun sank behind the trees, leaving an orange glow. 'It's great to have you back, just great,' Maeve said.

'It's great to be back,' I said, enjoying the sound of Ciaran and Dad playing ball in our garden. I was safe at last.

Twenty-Three

The next evening we were having our tea when the knock came to the door. It was Dad's old friend, Sergeant O'Connor. Dad pulled a chair out for him; Mam peered at him, her face white as the sheet she was folding. Slowly, she backed out of the room and stood in the hall, listening to them discussing the weather.

'You know what this visit is about, Jim,' Sergeant O'Connor said.

'I do and you're wasting your time, Tom, if you've come to take Stella back to the Magdalene Laundry. She should never have been there in the first place.'

'You realise that Stella and her baby are under the jurisdiction of the nuns, and therefore their property by law.'

'I know no such thing. Stella is our daughter and the baby is hers. They're living with us now, and Eileen and I are going to help Stella rear Holly while she completes her education.'

Sergeant O'Connor shook his head. 'I don't think that's possible, Jim.'

'You make it possible, Tom, because we're not parting with Holly. The nuns have no legal rights, but we'll adopt Holly ourselves if that's what it takes to hold on to her,' Dad said.

I almost cried out in surprise but managed to stop myself, coughing instead as the air caught in my throat.

Sergeant O'Connor looked from Dad to me, then took out his notebook. I watched him draw a line through my name. With a stroke of his pen he'd struck out the nuns, the laundry, the girls – all my links with that part of my past. Then he slipped his notebook back into his jacket pocket and got to his feet. He and Dad shook hands. 'That's that then, Jim,' he said, and turning to me he said, 'You're a lucky girl, Stella.'

Dad started his new job on a building site in Wicklow town, and Mam threw herself into her sewing. She sewed constantly, her head bent over her machine as she pushed a length of material forward, her fingers shaping it as it went, her eyes on the shuttle as it ran back and forth. She worked as if her whole life depended on it, and kept a notebook with lists of the names of her customers. She said she'd had enough of the Browns, when I asked her why she'd left them.

Ciaran, Holly and I went for walks in the evenings. We would go to the beach to collect shells from the seashore. Often he would wade into the freezing waves, his arm outstretched to grab at a gleaming object. We strolled along the railway path. New growth was everywhere, the tips of leaves promising an early spring. It was all the same as the previous years, yet in the space of time we'd been apart we'd both grown up alot. Ciaran was taller. His hair fell into his eyes, freckles spilled across his nose. One evening on the way up our street, Johnny Flynn, a neighbour's son, came to look into the pram. Holly was asleep.

'What's her name?' the boy asked.

'Holly,' Ciaran said proudly.

His mother came to her door. 'Come away from there, Johnny,' she called out to him, her hands on her hips. John went striding off, Ciaran looking after him.

The following Saturday, Maeve and I pushed the pram down to the beach. The breeze was cool; waves were gathering and breaking against the shore. Mary Brown and two of her pals were sitting on the wall near the rocks, their dark shapes hunched forward as if they were about to jump. As we drew near to them, Mary jumped down from the wall and faced me. 'What are you doing back here, Stella Wood? I thought you'd been packed off for good.'

'It's none of your business, Mary,' Maeve said.

Mary's face was peevish. 'You'd better go back to where you came from; we don't want scum like you in our town, do we girls?' she called up to the other two.

'No, we don't,' they chorused.

A lump rose in my throat. I felt sick. It was like a bad dream. In that instant all my hopes of starting afresh in Knocknacree vanished.

Maeve grasped my arm for reassurance. 'Come on, let's go home; it's going to rain.'

We turned our backs on the gunmetal sea and headed for home, their laughter ringing in our ears.

Dad said, 'Stella! What's the matter?' as soon as I walked in the door. I told him what had happened. He put his hand on my shoulder. 'Don't let them get you down,' he said, smiling to hide his fury.

Mam said, 'I knew this would happen.' She put her hands to her forehead as if to relieve the unbearable pressure in her head.

I fed Holly, put her down for the night, and went out into the darkening garden to get away from the stifling atmosphere in the kitchen. Their voices floated to me through the stillness. I watched them in the light of the kitchen, Dad's hand gripped firmly around Mam's waist, Mam's head tilted towards him. I could hear the rustle of Maeve's hens settling down for the night. The place seemed desolate; everywhere was still, as if waiting for me to leave.

The ripples of disapproval were spreading. Ciaran came home from school upset one day. He said that the other children in his class were saying bad things about me and calling me names. I looked at him standing at the kitchen table, his schoolbag hanging off of his shoulders, Mam's hand pressed into his back consolingly, and felt sick.

I spent most days at home, listening to the radio, helping Mam, not daring to show my face in the town. There were often arguments between Mam and Dad at night, in their bedroom. I would turn my face into the pillow, trying not to listen to them. In the mornings Mam's head would be bowed, as if she found to hard to face the day.

A few days later there was a knock on the door. When I answered it, Leo was standing there, smiling.

'Leo!'

'I met your Dad in the town. He said you were back.'

'Yes. I think I gave him the excuse he needed to come home.'

'Is everything OK?' he asked, looking at me, waiting.

I shook my head. 'It's hard – the gossip seems to grow and spread. I'm never going to be allowed to forget what happened,' I said, my voice cracking.

I made us tea. We talked about his job. After a while the conversation turned to Charles. 'His family are selling up, moving.'

'Oh! Where to?'

'Dublin.'

'They can't take the gossip?'

Leo looked out of the window. 'No.'

'That's why I can't stay here,' I said with finality.

Leo looked at me. I told him everything; about meeting

Mary Brown and the others at the beach, and about what happened when Johnny Flynn's mother caught him looking into the pram, and about the name-calling Ciaran had to put up with in school because of me. I told him that Irene had come round to see me, but that she hadn't offered me my job in the café back, and that I hadn't been to the town, hadn't talked to any of the neighbours. 'People don't know what to say to me. They're shocked, ashamed, so they shun me.'

There was pity in Leo's face as he said, 'That's the price you have to pay for living in a small town.'

'I'm thinking of going back to Auntie Nora's, then they won't have to worry about me contaminating their town any more. Anyway, I don't feel part of Knocknacree any more, and, for the first time in my life, I don't care about the place. It's all too painful.'

Leo nodded.

I gazed out of the window, thinking about the fields, the woods and the hills, remembering my childhood: running about in the fields, climbing trees, being free.

'I think Charles felt the same way about Knocknacree.'

'I know.'

'You don't have to worry about me running off. I'll be round to visit you in Bray often, unless you don't want me to come?' He looked at me anxiously.

'Of course I'll want to see you, Leo. You're my best friend.'

A smile of relief spread over his face.

* * *

The open suitcase stirred up so many memories that I had to turn away from it. Mam was sitting on the edge of my bed, carefully folding my neatly ironed clothes into it. I was preparing to leave home once more.

Dad came in. 'Are you ready?' he asked.

'Yes,' Mam said. 'I'll make you a cup of tea before you hit the road.'

'I didn't expect things to be perfect, but I didn't think it would come to this. I thought they'd forget, leave us in peace,' Dad said, blowing on his tea.

'How could they, with Holly here as a constant reminder,' Mam said.

'I thought that with everything that had happened we'd come through,' he sighed.

'Come on now, Stella,' Dad said, ushering me out the door.

Mam and Ciaran stood at the gate; the neighbours down the road came to their doors to watch.

'We'll pay you a visit soon,' Mam said, giving my shoulder a squeeze as I got into the passenger seat of the car.

'So here we are setting off on another journey,' Dad said, as cheerfully as he could.

I was glad to be going. The Knocknacree I'd known had changed. It wasn't part of my life any more. I liked the thought of going to live in Bray. Dad had arranged for me to attend the vocational school there the following

September, and Auntie Nora had said that she'd love to have us come and stay. Even Uncle Billy was quite willing to have us back again, especially as Dad would be paying for our keep and the trouble with the law was over.

Twenty-Four

It was Holly's first birthday. Auntie Nora had decided to have a party for her. She saw this event as an opportunity for a family reunion. Mam, Dad, Ciaran and Maeve were the first guests to arrive. They hugged me, then Holly. Ciaran took her out of my arms and carried her inside, eager to play with her. Maeve looked tall and elegant in a new blue coat that Mam had made for her as a birthday present. Mam greeted Auntie Nora with a formal handshake. I could sense the tension between them.

Marie was next to arrive. After I'd gone back to Bray, I'd started writing to her, telling her all my news. When I'd told Auntie Nora about Marie – trapped at the convent, she'd pulled strings and found her a job as a housekeeper at the Bray Arms, the new hotel on the seafront. She looked prettier than ever with her hair pulled back into a ponytail and a green-and-white check coat. She'd brought a huge teddy bear for Holly.

Dad sat between Auntie Nora and Uncle Billy. Mam sat on Uncle Billy's left. Ciaran sat next to Holly in her highchair and clowned around with her. She laughed at him, showing off her two new frilly teeth. Marie took the seat on Holly's other side, Maeve sat beside me.

Uncle Billy said Grace. 'Bless us, O Lord, and these thy gifts, which of thy bounty we are about to receive through Christ Our Lord, Amen.'

'Amen,' we chorused.

Uncle Billy carved the joint of beef. Auntie Nora served the steaming vegetables and creamed potatoes. Dad poured the wine. 'Have a glass, it'll do you good,' he coaxed Marie.

'No thanks, I'll stick with the lemonade,' she said.

It was so good to see her, though it felt strange, like an ache or something.

Uncle Billy raised his glass and toasted Holly. 'Here's to a special baby, on her first birthday, and what a lovely baby she is,' he said proudly.

'Hear, hear,' they chorused.

Dad got to his feet. 'I would like to take this opportunity to thank Nora and Billy for taking such good care of her this past year.'

There was a clinking of glasses. Auntie Nora said, 'Oh, it's wonderful to have them living with us, isn't it, Billy?'

Uncle Billy said, in a subdued voice, 'The house would be very quiet without them. I might even get a night's sleep.'

There was a ripple of laughter. Mam stared at her plate as if she was feeling left out.

254

Leo arrived and apologised for being late. 'Charles sent this for Holly.'

I took the huge parcel in my hands and carried it into the kitchen. It was a doll and pram. There was a card with a big number one on it. Charles had written on it, 'You only get one life, Holly. Make it a good one.' Enclosed was a photograph of Charles looking happy and handsome, his eyes gazing out towards the sea, the wind blowing back his hair.

'How is he?' I asked Leo.

'He's doing well. He loves living in Boston, according to his mother. He's going to stay on and attend college there. His father hasn't forgiven him for this latest vanishing trick.'

A cold shiver ran down my spine. For a moment I couldn't speak. Leo put his arm round me. 'It's what he wants, Stella.' He was never happy here.

'I didn't know that.' Then I didn't know much about Charles. In the past year I'd hardly seen him, and he certainly didn't confide in me. 'Was it because of me and Holly?'

'No. Charles had problems at home. He didn't talk about them. He kept his secrets.'

Maeve perked up when she saw Leo. She kept her eyes on him as he went round the table shaking hands with everyone. Later we sat around, opening Holly's presents. Among them was a pretty pink dress with a birthday card signed, 'From your loving friend, Sister

Angela.' My eyes blurred as I thought of her kindly face.

I don't know what the future holds for Holly and me, but with the support of my family, I know I'll be able to complete my education. I'd like to study medicine, become a doctor and specialise in helping unmarried mothers with their unwanted pregnancies. Leo says he will help me with my studies, so, who knows, it might happen.

I looked around. All of the people that I loved most in the world were here with me, as one big family, just like the old days. It felt good. I felt very lucky.

Epilogue

It's a warm summer evening. The house is quiet, Holly is asleep and I'm out in the garden, revising. The Inter-Cert examinations are starting tomorrow and I'm very nervous. Uncle Billy has gone to the pub for his usual pint. Auntie Nora is taking a well-deserved, relaxing bath.

In a fortnight's time I'll be working in Dave's café for the summer. Already, the strand has a new look to it. The hotels and guesthouses that lined the Esplanade are repainted in bright colours for the coming season. Window boxes are being planted out. Soon, the kiosks will be selling ice cream and the bars and cafés will be in full swing with the holidaymakers.

Mam and Dad have bought a house in Wicklow town to be near Dad's work. Ciaran has got on to the under twelves' football team and is delighted with himself. I'll be able to visit them often, but I won't go and live with them. I'll stay in Bray and finish my schooling. I like the school. The teachers are nice and the boys and girls are friendly. Auntie Nora is wonderful with Holly. Uncle

Billy adores her. Even the neighbours have accepted us now that we are permanent fixtures.

As for Charles? I haven't heard from him and neither has Leo. His memory lives on in Holly with her blue eyes and her quick, mischievous smile, but when I look at her now the sharp ache of loss has gone.

I'll get up very early in the morning and do some revision before I go to school, just as I do every day. I'll try not to be too nervous when I go in to sit my exams. In the evening I'll take Holly for a walk, like I do most evenings. We'll gaze out at the sea, watch the waves chasing one another to the shore, and listen to the squawking seagulls.

As I breathe in the sea air I'll offer up a prayer of thanks for the gift of my daughter, and for my freedom, and for Leo, like I do every day. Leo has been a true friend – more than a friend, since my return to Bray. I go out with him when I can. He is very kind to me.

One evening last week, when we were out for a walk, we stopped at the top of Bray Head.

'This is where you rescued me,' I said to him, looking towards the woods. 'I'll always be grateful,' I added.

He smiled. 'I'm glad you came back.'

'So am I,' I said, telling him how wonderful it was to be able to go wherever I wanted to, whenever I felt like it, without fear.

Leo slipped his arm round me. 'I'm happy when I'm with you, Stella.'

'And I'm happy when I'm with you too,' I smiled.

He moved closer. 'I was afraid that having been hurt by Charles may have put you off . . . me . . . men . . . for life.'

'No, it hasn't,' I laughed.

Suddenly Leo was very serious. 'Stella, I want to take care of you and Holly, and not just now — always. I'm quite willing to be second-best.'

'Leo! You could never be second-best; we have so much in common . . . I couldn't imagine a world without you in it.'

He took me in his arms. 'I love you, Stella.'

As he said it I realised that I loved him, too. Properly loved him.

As we strolled home, Leo said, 'When I'm qualified I'm going to ask you to marry me.'

I thought he was joking, but he stopped and asked me straight out. 'Would you, Stella?' The way he looked at me made me certain that he really meant it — but I couldn't say yes, not there and then.

In a shaky voice I said, 'I'd like to be a doctor too, Leo, and help unmarried mothers so that they won't have to end up in a Magdalene laundry like I did.'

He wrapped his arms around me tightly. 'I understand, and I'll wait for you for as long as it takes.'

We kissed. I closed my eyes. As long as I live, I shall always remember that kiss. As we clung together all around was quiet and still, with just the beating of our hearts. When I opened my eyes ages later, the sun was shining on the water and felt happier than I could have ever imagined.

We continued on, hand in hand, talking about the years ahead. They ought to be exciting years, because I hope we'll spend them together, for always.

He Wishes For The Cloths of Heaven

Had I the heavens' embroidered cloths,
Enwrought with golden and silver light,
The blue and the dim and the dark cloths
Of night and light and the half-light,
I would spread the cloths under your feet:
But I, being poor, have only my dreams;
I have spread my dreams under your feet;
Tread softly because you tread on my dreams.

W.B. Yeats

Acknowledgements

My special thanks to the following for their help with the writing of the book: Lindsey Earner, PHD, for sharing her specialised knowledge on unmarried mothers and her valuable time with me; my 'penitent' friend who bravely told me her sad story; Marguerite Faulkner, and all the staff at Ballywaltrim Library for help with research, and kindness; June Flanagan for her feedback and instructive criticism; Mary Markham, Wendy O'Donoghue, and all my artist friends for their loyalty, friendship, and fun; Sheila Barrett, Alison Dye, Renata Ahrens-Kramer, Phil MaCarthy, Cecilia McGovern, and Julie Parsons for their important criticisms and enthusiasm.

I'm particularly grateful to Emily Thomas for her expert editing, insights and encouragement; Jonathan Lloyd for his unflagging support; my family for unstinting love, friendship and inspiration.